POKÉMON™

BLACK AND WHITE

VOL. 4

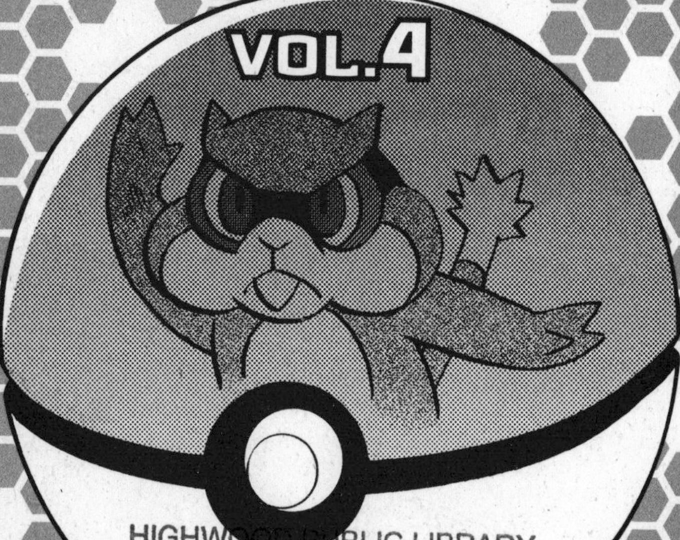

Story by HIDENORI KUSAKA
Art by SATOSHI YAMAMOTO

Pokémon Black and White
Volume 4
VIZ Kids Edition

Story by HIDENORI KUSAKA
Art by SATOSHI YAMAMOTO

© 2011 Pokémon.
© 1995–2011 Nintendo/Creatures Inc./GAME FREAK inc.
TM and ® and character names are trademarks of Nintendo.
© 1997 Hidenori KUSAKA and Satoshi YAMAMOTO/Shogakukan
All rights reserved.
Original Japanese edition "POCKET MONSTER SPECIAL"
published by SHOGAKUKAN Inc.

English Adaptation / Annette Roman
Translation / Tetsuichiro Miyaki
Touch-up & Lettering / Susan Daigle-Leach
Design / Fawn Lau
Cover Colorist / Laurence Menor
Editor / Annette Roman

Printed in the U.S.A.

Published by VIZ Media, LLC
P.O. Box 77010
San Francisco, CA 94107

10 9 8 7 6 5 4 3 2 1
First printing, November 2011

www.vizkids.com

www.viz.com

POKÉMON

BLACK AND WHITE

VOL.4

THE STORY THUS FAR!

Pokémon Trainer Black is exploring the mysterious Unova region with his brand-new Pokédex. Pokémon Trainer White runs a thriving talent agency for performing Pokémon. White hires Black to work for her, but he's always running off to fight Gym battles while she is all business!

BLACK'S dream is to win the Pokémon League!

WHITE'S dream is to make her Tepig Gigi a star!

Black's Tepig, TEP, and White's Tepig, GIGI, get along like peanut butter and jelly!

Black's Munna, MUSHA, helps him think clearly by temporarily "eating" his dream.

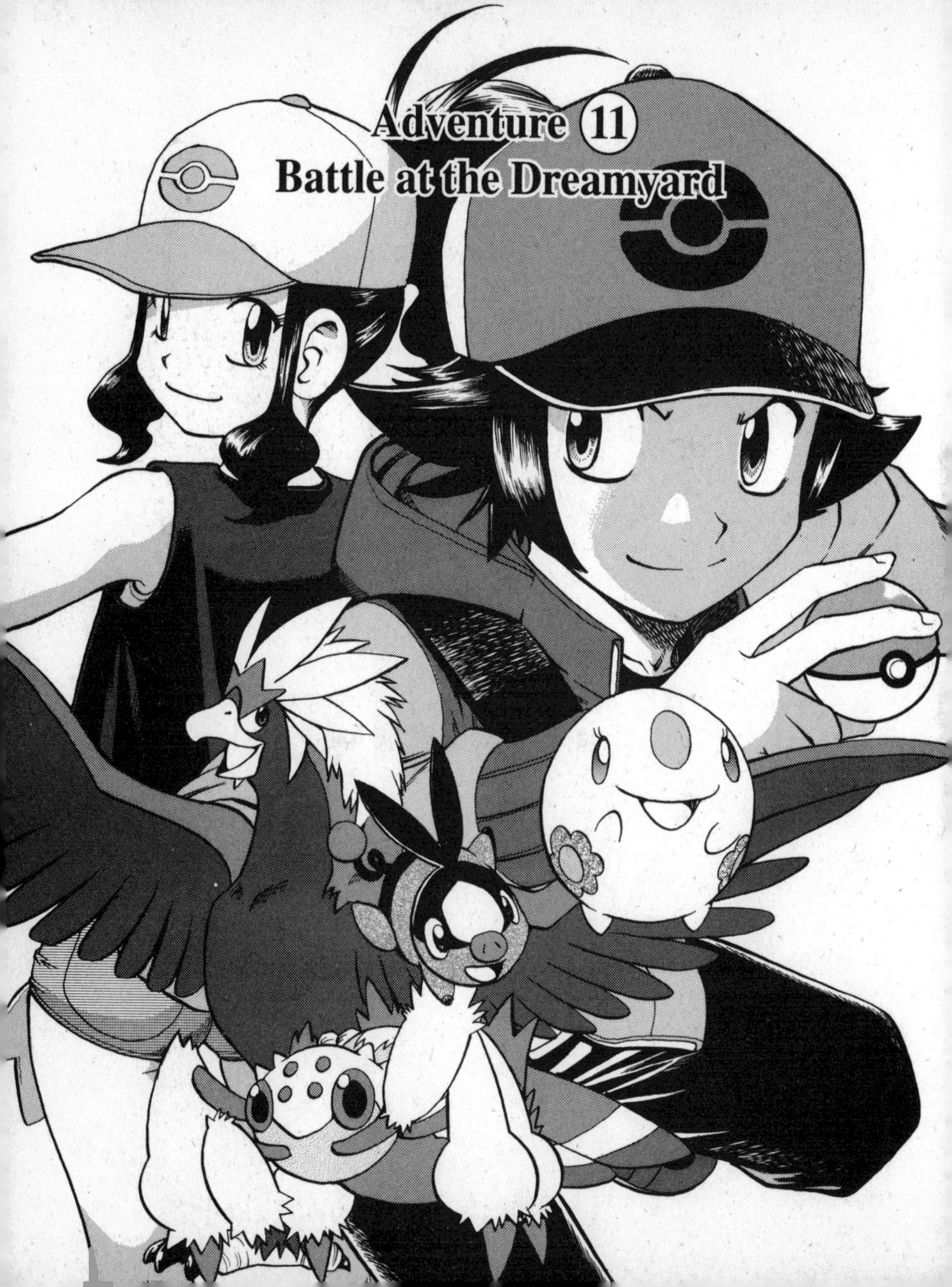
Adventure 11
Battle at the Dreamyard

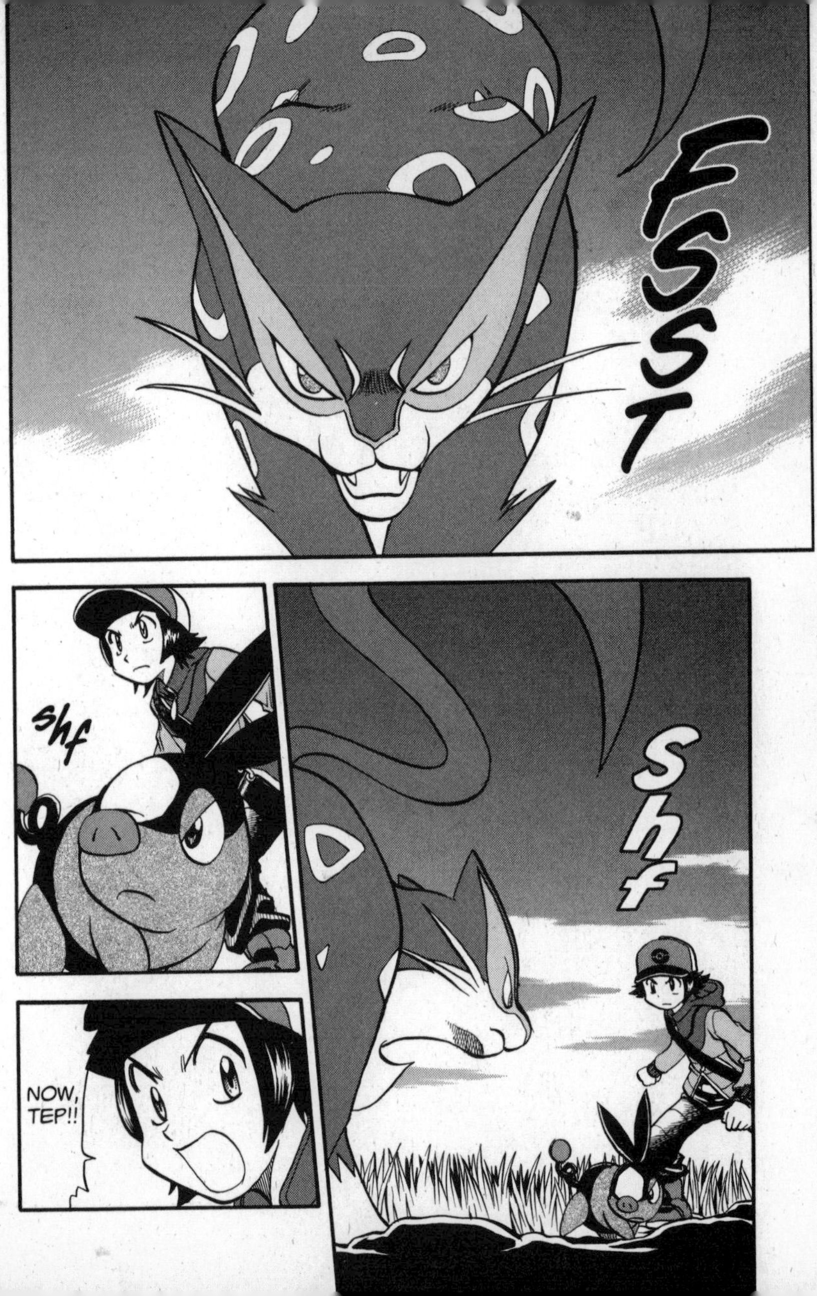
FSST
Shf
Shf
NOW, TEP!!

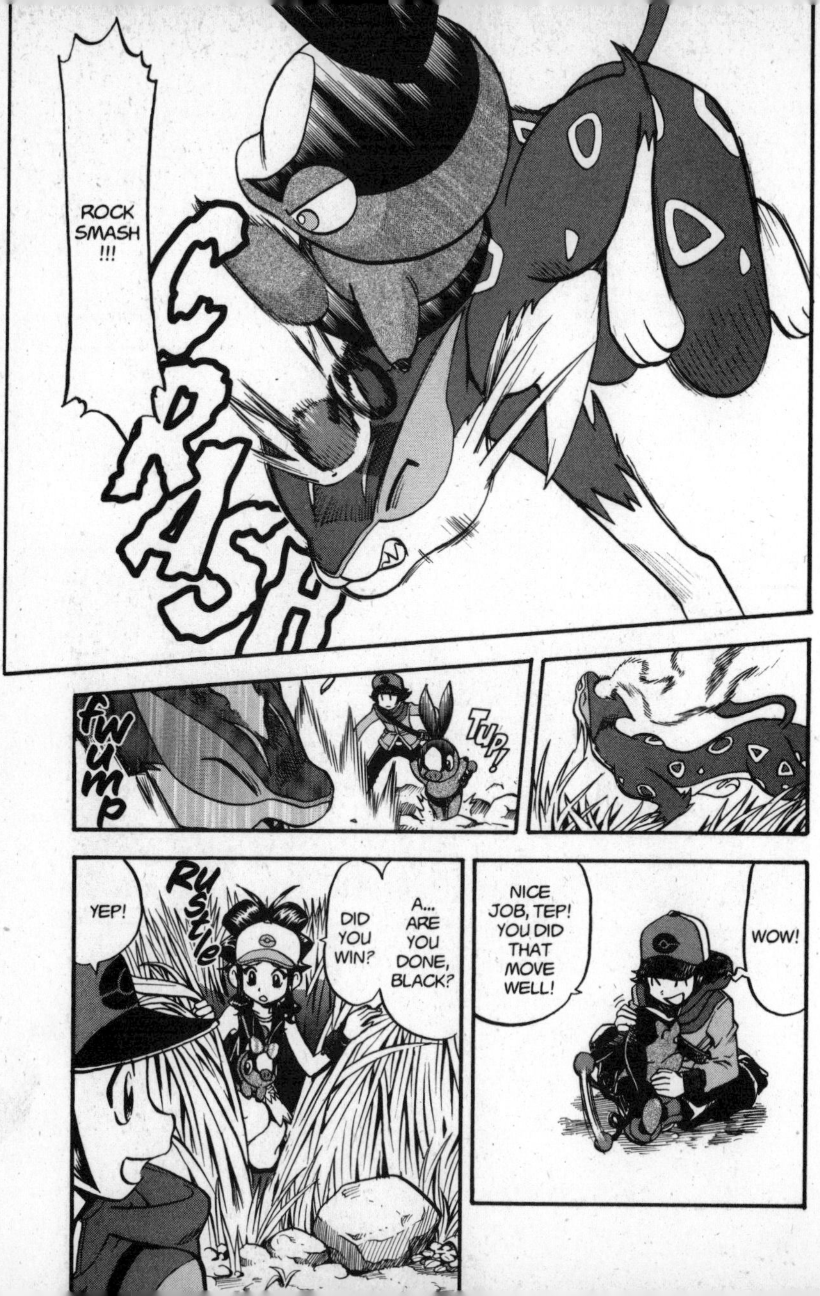
ROCK SMASH !!!
CRASH
TUP!
fwump
WOW!
NICE JOB, TEP! YOU DID THAT MOVE WELL!
A... ARE YOU DONE, BLACK?
DID YOU WIN?
RUSTLE
YEP!

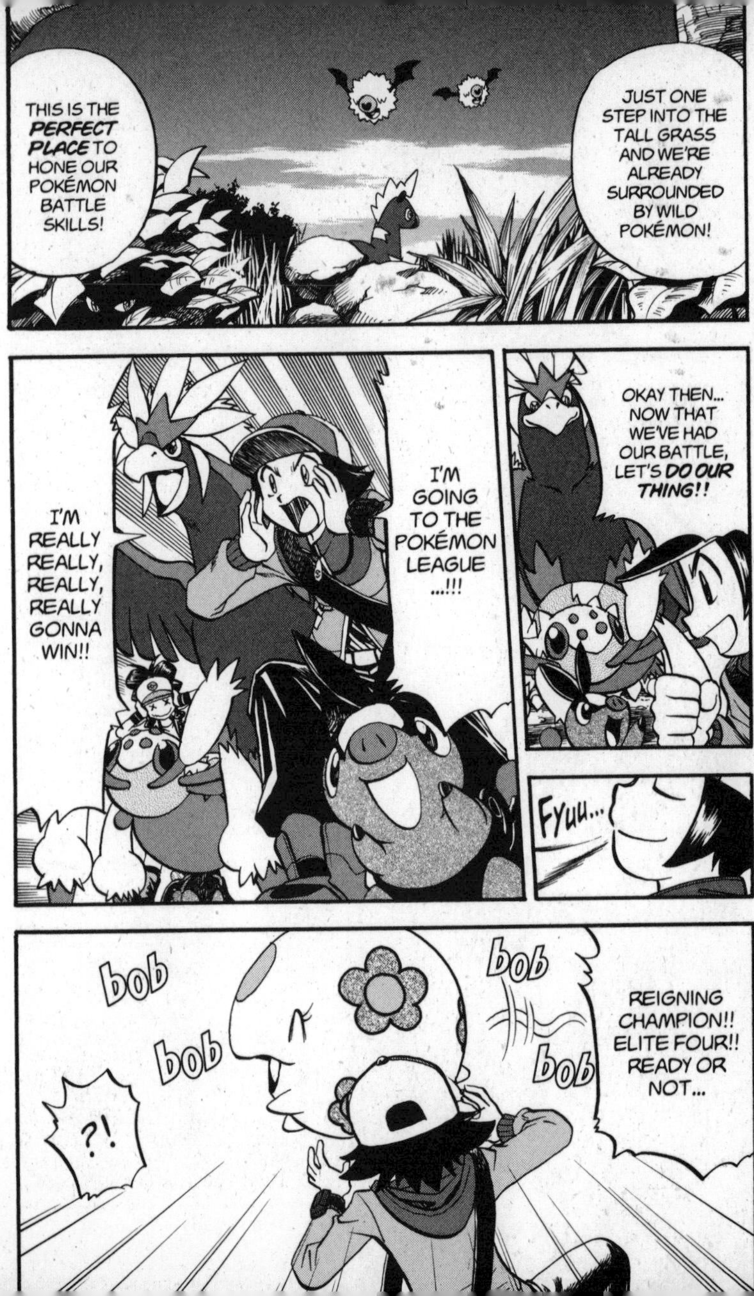
THIS IS THE PERFECT PLACE TO HONE OUR POKÉMON BATTLE SKILLS!
JUST ONE STEP INTO THE TALL GRASS AND WE'RE ALREADY SURROUNDED BY WILD POKÉMON!
I'M REALLY REALLY, REALLY, REALLY GONNA WIN!!
I'M GOING TO THE POKÉMON LEAGUE ...!!!
OKAY THEN... NOW THAT WE'VE HAD OUR BATTLE, LET'S DO OUR THING!!
Fyuu...
bob
bob
bob
bob
?!
REIGNING CHAMPION!! ELITE FOUR!! READY OR NOT...

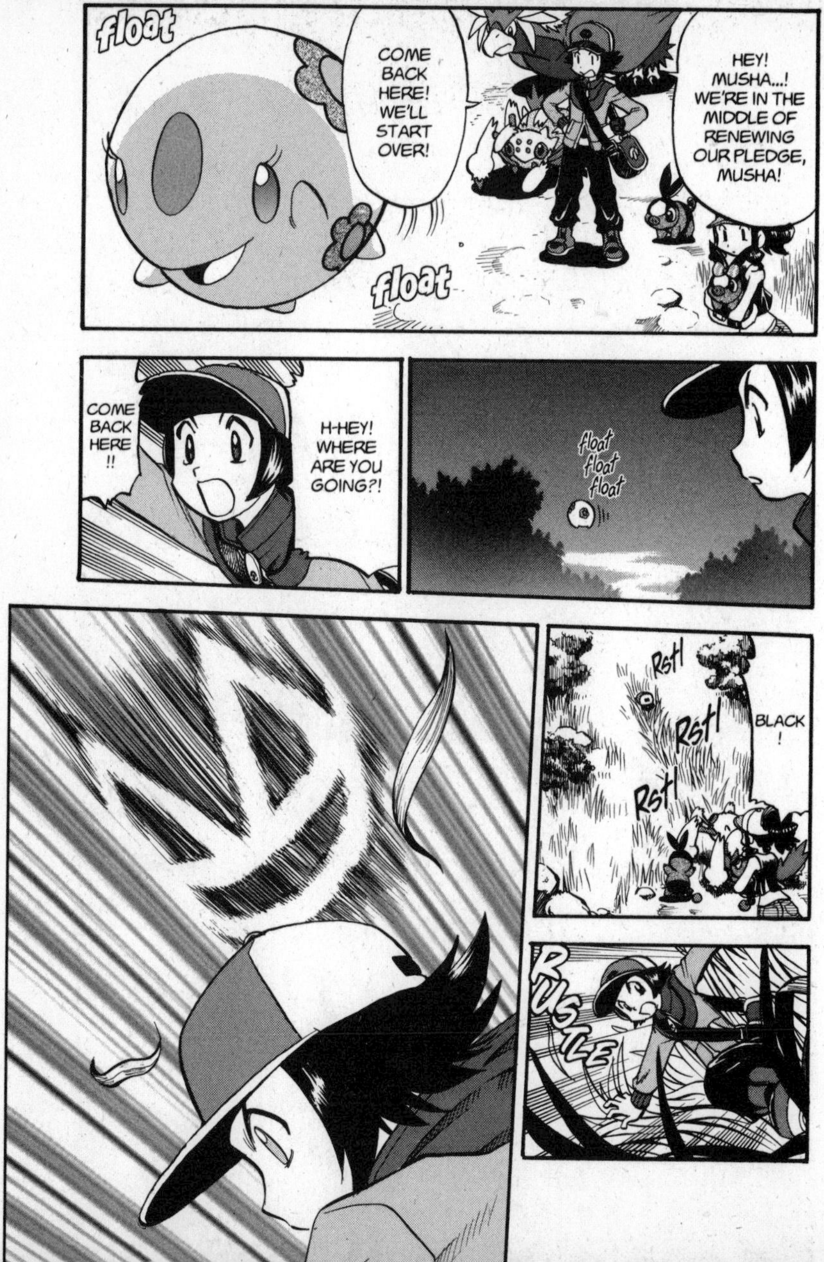
float
COME BACK HERE! WE'LL START OVER!
HEY! MUSHA...! WE'RE IN THE MIDDLE OF RENEWING OUR PLEDGE, MUSHA!
float
COME BACK HERE !!
H-HEY! WHERE ARE YOU GOING?!
float float float
Rstl
Rstl
Rstl
BLACK !
RUSTLE

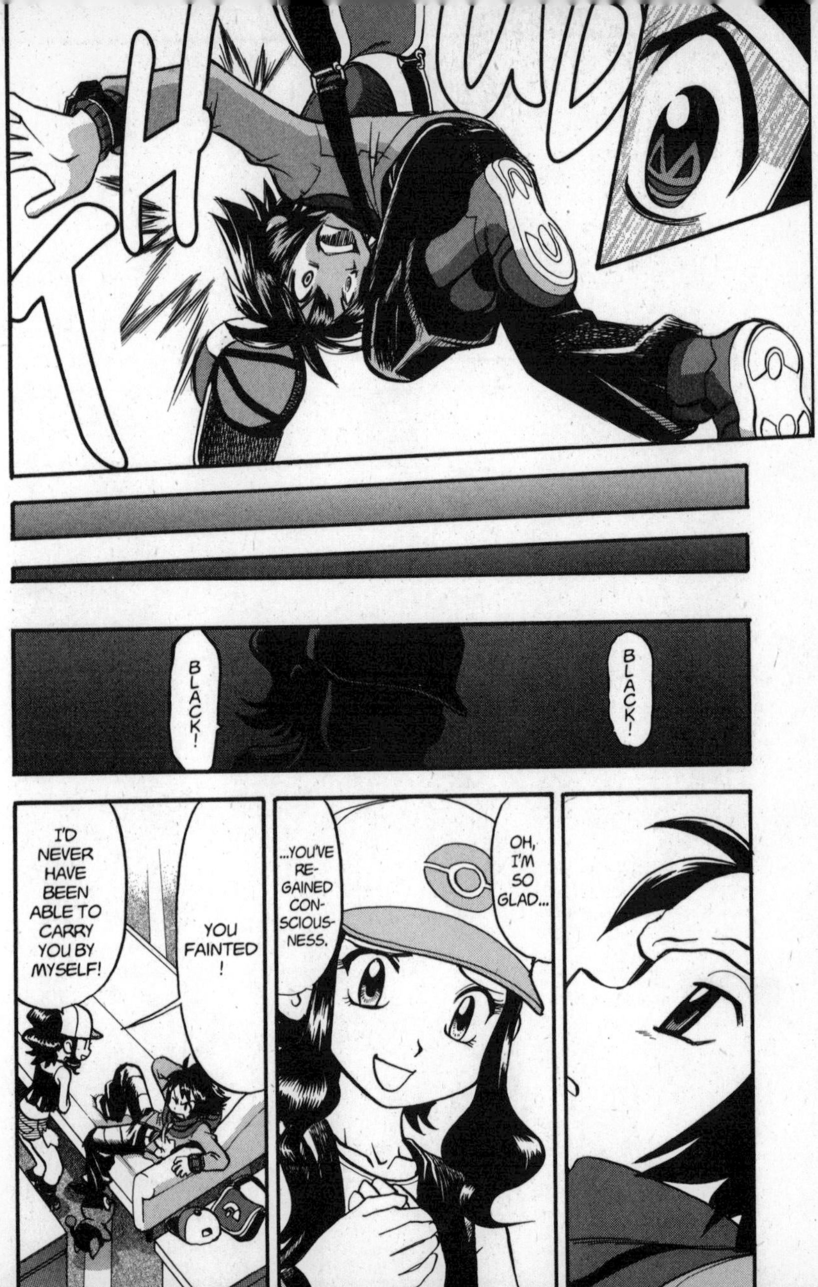
BLACK!
BLACK!
OH, I'M SO GLAD...
...YOU'VE RE-GAINED CONSCIOUS-NESS.
YOU FAINTED!
I'D NEVER HAVE BEEN ABLE TO CARRY YOU BY MYSELF!

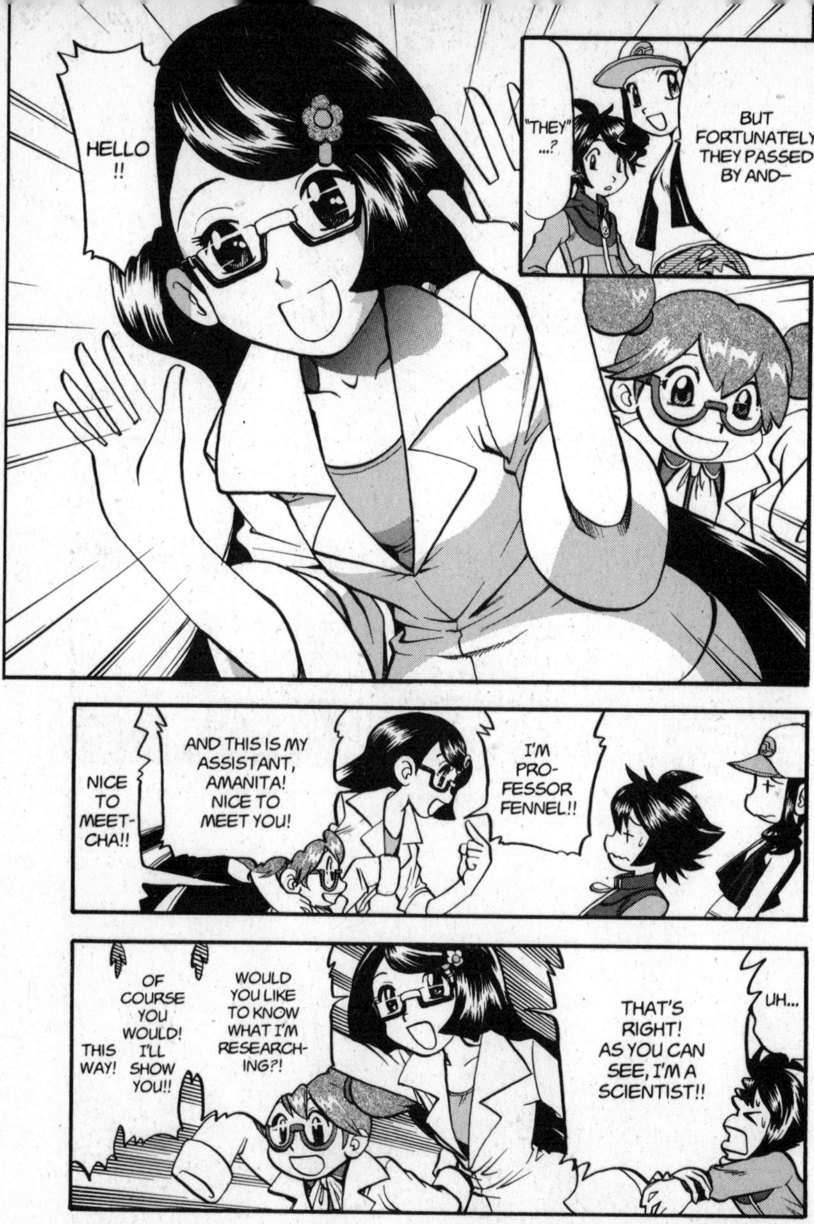
BUT FORTUNATELY THEY PASSED BY AND—
"THEY" ...?
HELLO !!
I'M PROFESSOR FENNEL!!
AND THIS IS MY ASSISTANT, AMANITA! NICE TO MEET YOU!
NICE TO MEET-CHA!!
UH...
THAT'S RIGHT! AS YOU CAN SEE, I'M A SCIENTIST!!
WOULD YOU LIKE TO KNOW WHAT I'M RESEARCH-ING?!
OF COURSE YOU WOULD! I'LL SHOW YOU!!
THIS WAY!

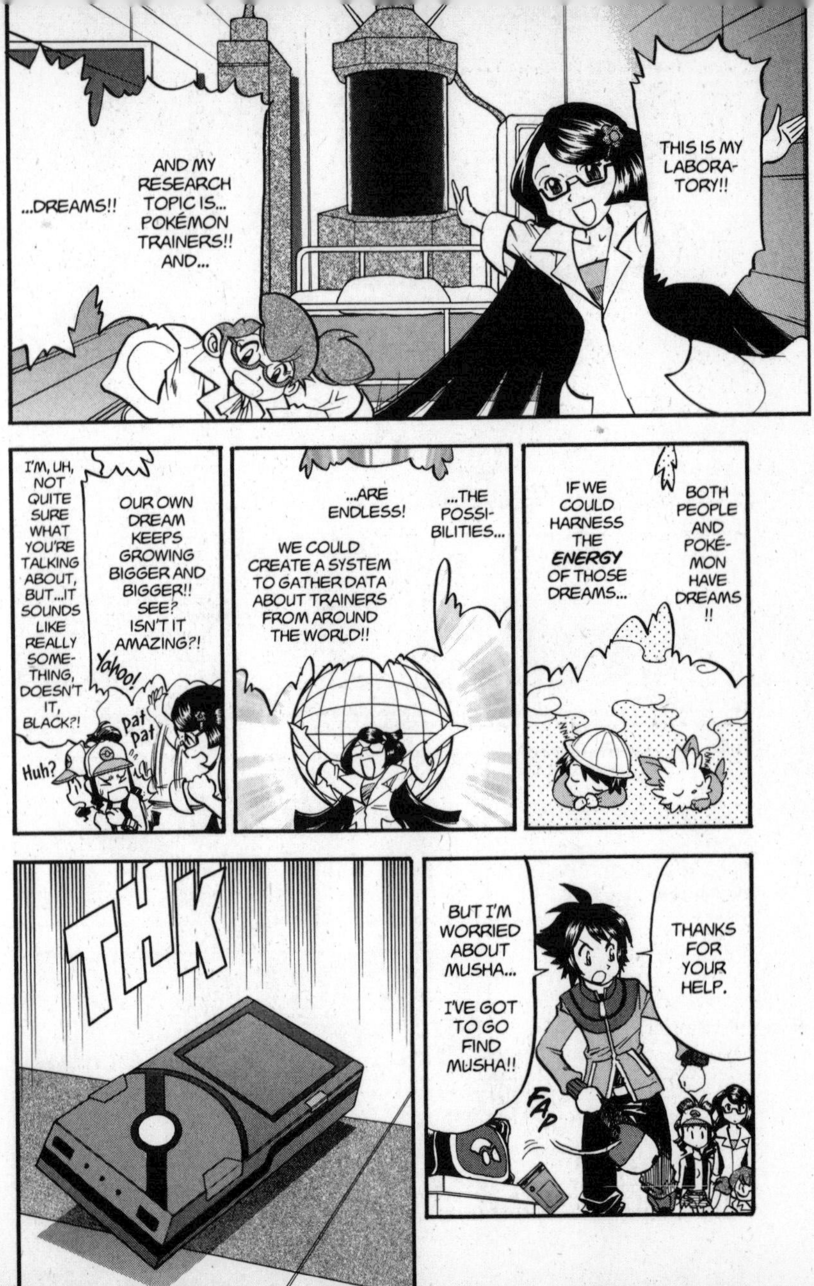
THIS IS MY LABORATORY!!
AND MY RESEARCH TOPIC IS... POKÉMON TRAINERS!! AND...
...DREAMS!!
BOTH PEOPLE AND POKÉMON HAVE DREAMS!!
IF WE COULD HARNESS THE ENERGY OF THOSE DREAMS...
...THE POSSIBILITIES...
...ARE ENDLESS!
WE COULD CREATE A SYSTEM TO GATHER DATA ABOUT TRAINERS FROM AROUND THE WORLD!!
OUR OWN DREAM KEEPS GROWING BIGGER AND BIGGER!! SEE? ISN'T IT AMAZING?!
I'M, UH, NOT QUITE SURE WHAT YOU'RE TALKING ABOUT, BUT...IT SOUNDS LIKE REALLY SOMETHING, DOESN'T IT, BLACK?!
Yahoo!
pat pat
Huh?
THANKS FOR YOUR HELP.
BUT I'M WORRIED ABOUT MUSHA...
I'VE GOT TO GO FIND MUSHA!!
FAP
THK

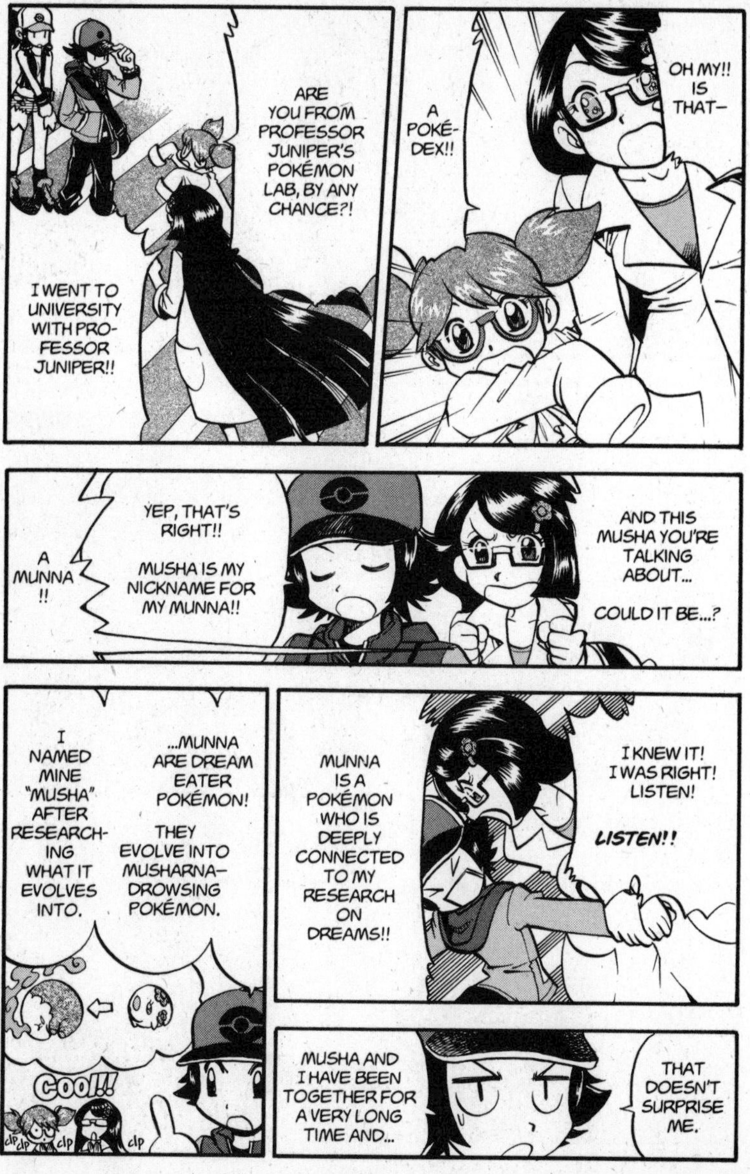

ARE YOU FROM PROFESSOR JUNIPER'S POKÉMON LAB, BY ANY CHANCE?!
I WENT TO UNIVERSITY WITH PRO-FESSOR JUNIPER!!
OH MY!! IS THAT—
A POKÉ-DEX!!
A MUNNA !!
YEP, THAT'S RIGHT!!
MUSHA IS MY NICKNAME FOR MY MUNNA!!
AND THIS MUSHA YOU'RE TALKING ABOUT...
COULD IT BE...?
I NAMED MINE "MUSHA" AFTER RESEARCH-ING WHAT IT EVOLVES INTO.
...MUNNA ARE DREAM EATER POKÉMON!
THEY EVOLVE INTO MUSHARNA-DROWSING POKÉMON.
Cool!!
clp clp clp clp
MUNNA IS A POKÉMON WHO IS DEEPLY CONNECTED TO MY RESEARCH ON DREAMS!!
I KNEW IT! I WAS RIGHT! LISTEN!
LISTEN!!
MUSHA AND I HAVE BEEN TOGETHER FOR A VERY LONG TIME AND...
THAT DOESN'T SURPRISE ME.

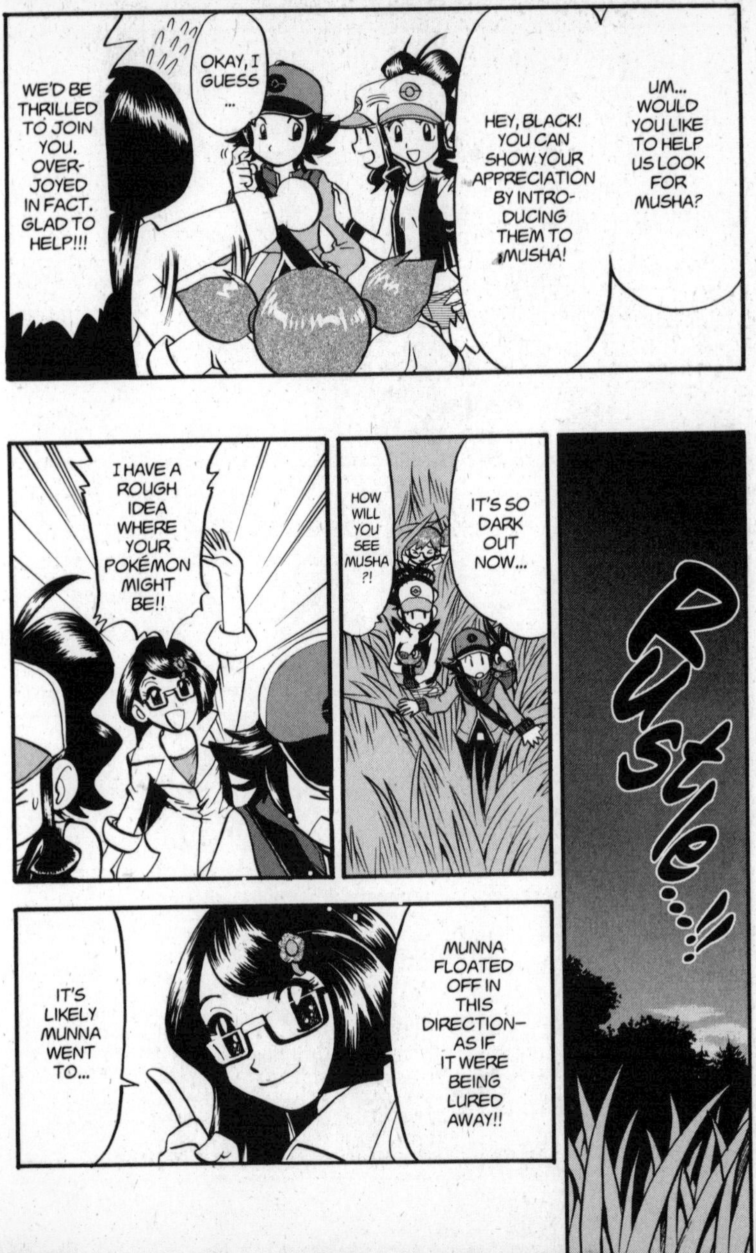
UM... WOULD YOU LIKE TO HELP US LOOK FOR MUSHA?
HEY, BLACK! YOU CAN SHOW YOUR APPRECIATION BY INTRODUCING THEM TO MUSHA!
OKAY, I GUESS ...
WE'D BE THRILLED TO JOIN YOU. OVERJOYED IN FACT. GLAD TO HELP!!!
RUSTLE...!!
IT'S SO DARK OUT NOW...
HOW WILL YOU SEE MUSHA?!
I HAVE A ROUGH IDEA WHERE YOUR POKÉMON MIGHT BE!!
MUNNA FLOATED OFF IN THIS DIRECTION—AS IF IT WERE BEING LURED AWAY!!
IT'S LIKELY MUNNA WENT TO...

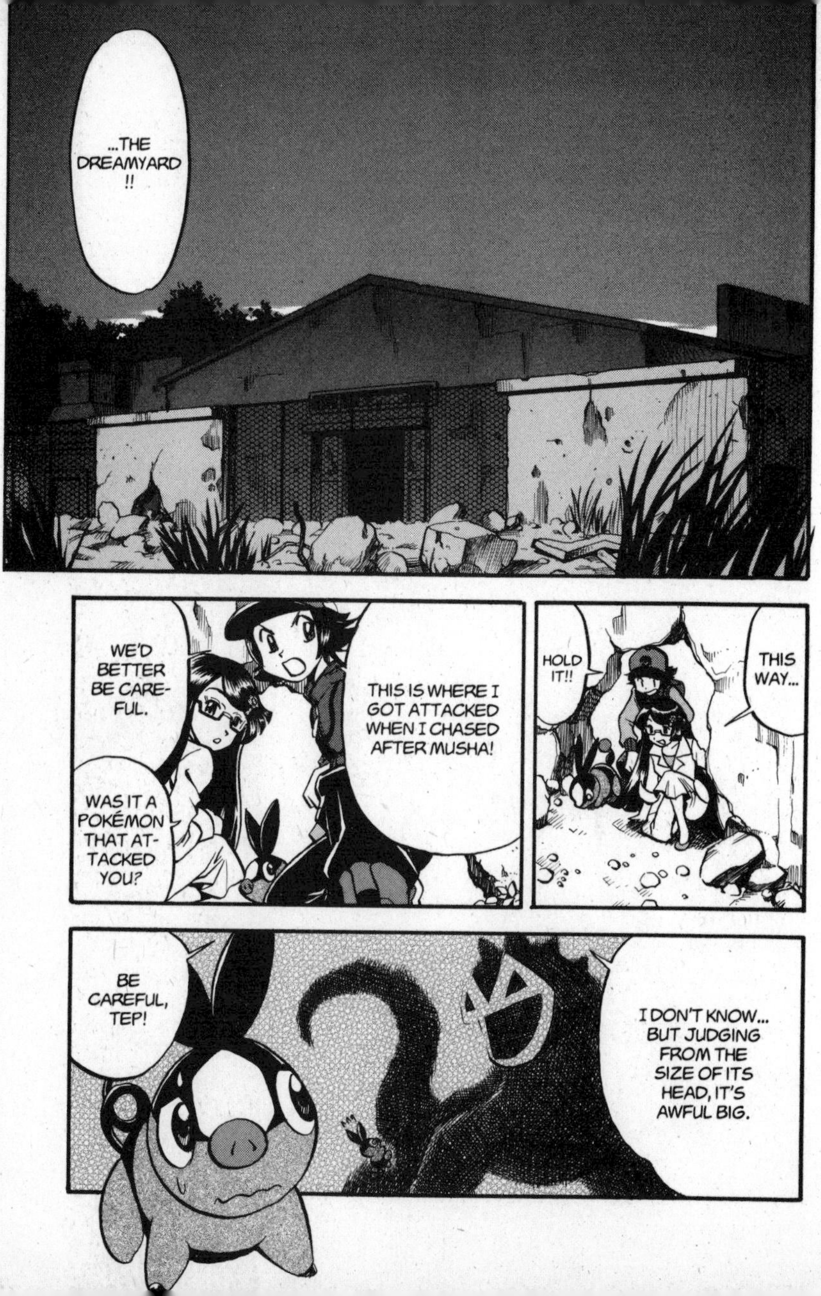
...THE DREAMYARD !!
WE'D BETTER BE CARE-FUL.
THIS IS WHERE I GOT ATTACKED WHEN I CHASED AFTER MUSHA!
WAS IT A POKÉMON THAT AT-TACKED YOU?
THIS WAY...
HOLD IT!!
I DON'T KNOW... BUT JUDGING FROM THE SIZE OF ITS HEAD, IT'S AWFUL BIG.
BE CAREFUL, TEP!

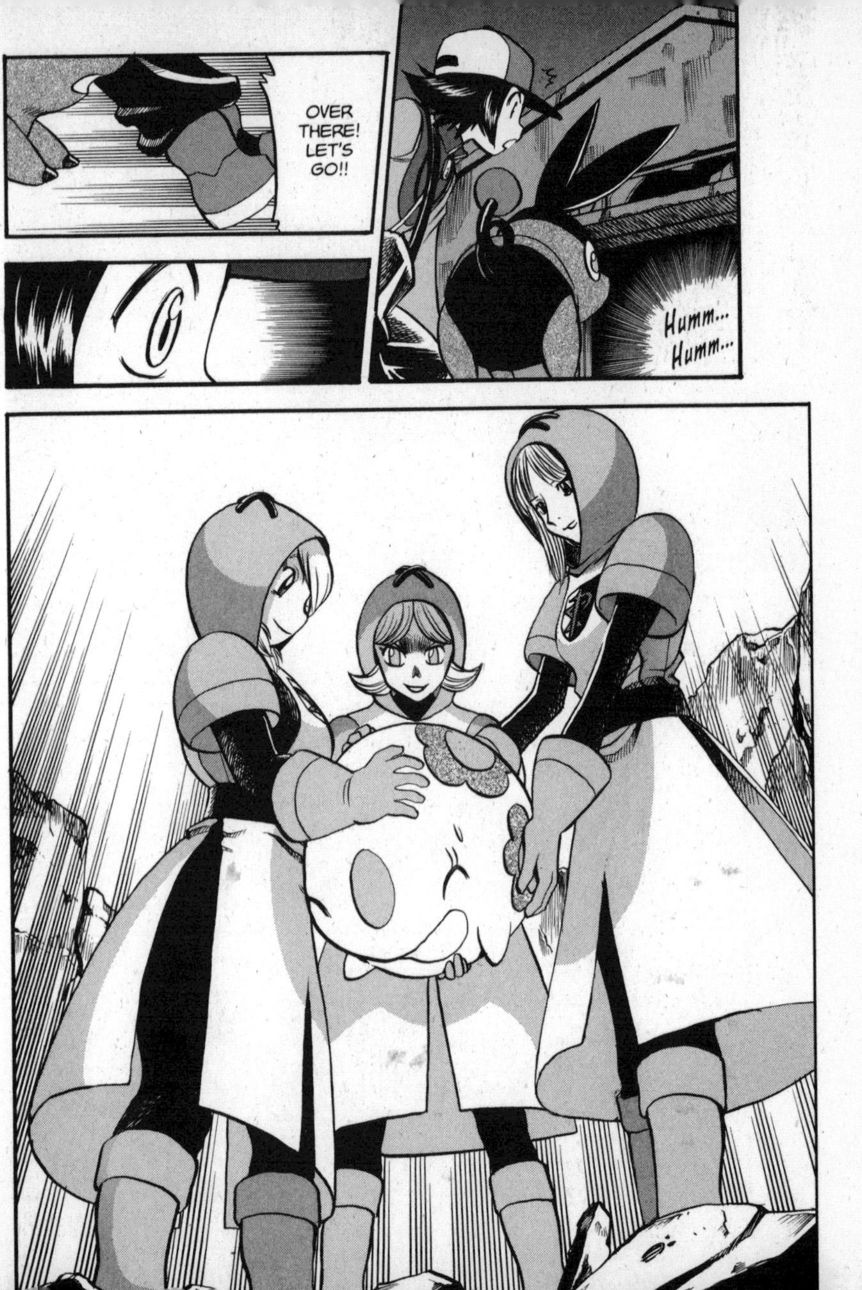
OVER THERE! LET'S GO!!
Humm... Humm...

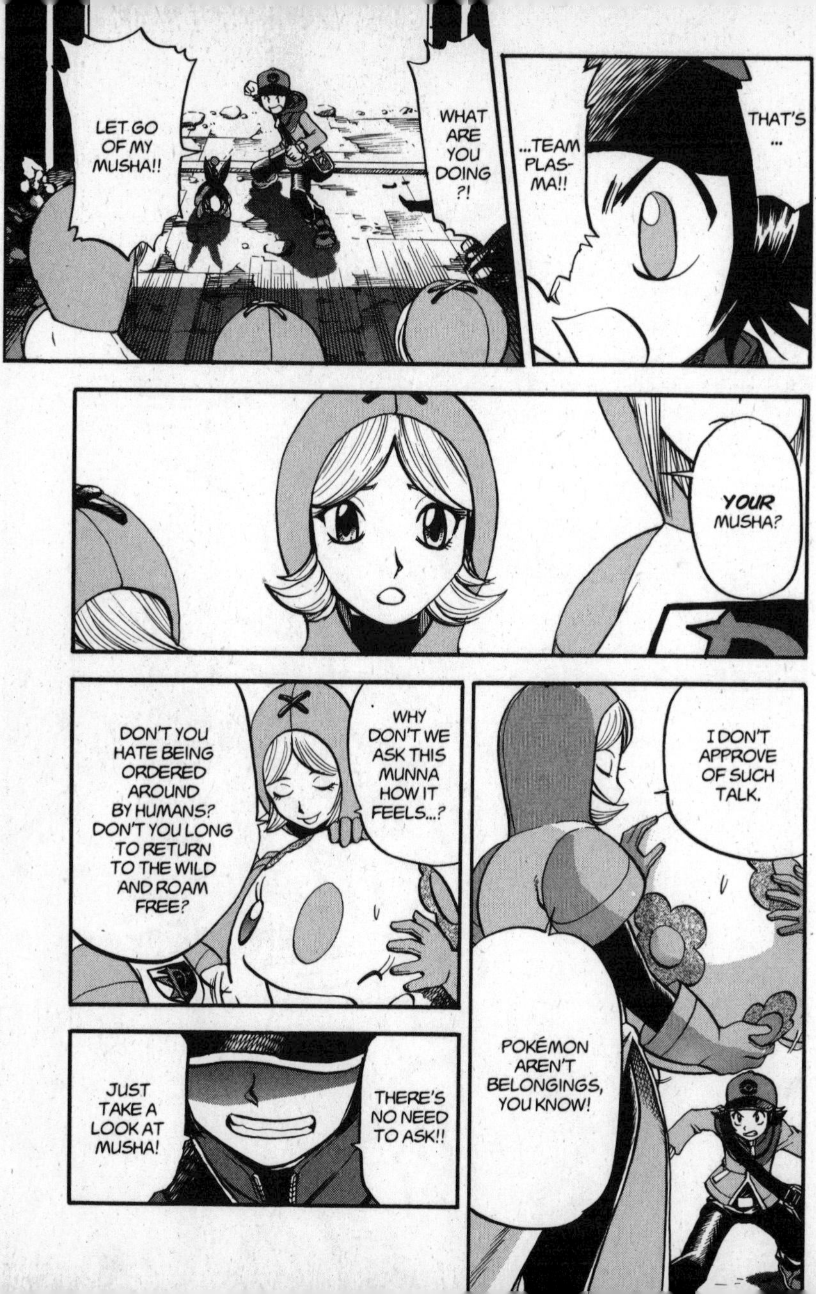
LET GO OF MY MUSHA!!
WHAT ARE YOU DOING?!
...TEAM PLASMA!!
THAT'S ...
YOUR MUSHA?
DON'T YOU HATE BEING ORDERED AROUND BY HUMANS? DON'T YOU LONG TO RETURN TO THE WILD AND ROAM FREE?
WHY DON'T WE ASK THIS MUNNA HOW IT FEELS...?
I DON'T APPROVE OF SUCH TALK.
JUST TAKE A LOOK AT MUSHA!
THERE'S NO NEED TO ASK!!
POKÉMON AREN'T BELONGINGS, YOU KNOW!

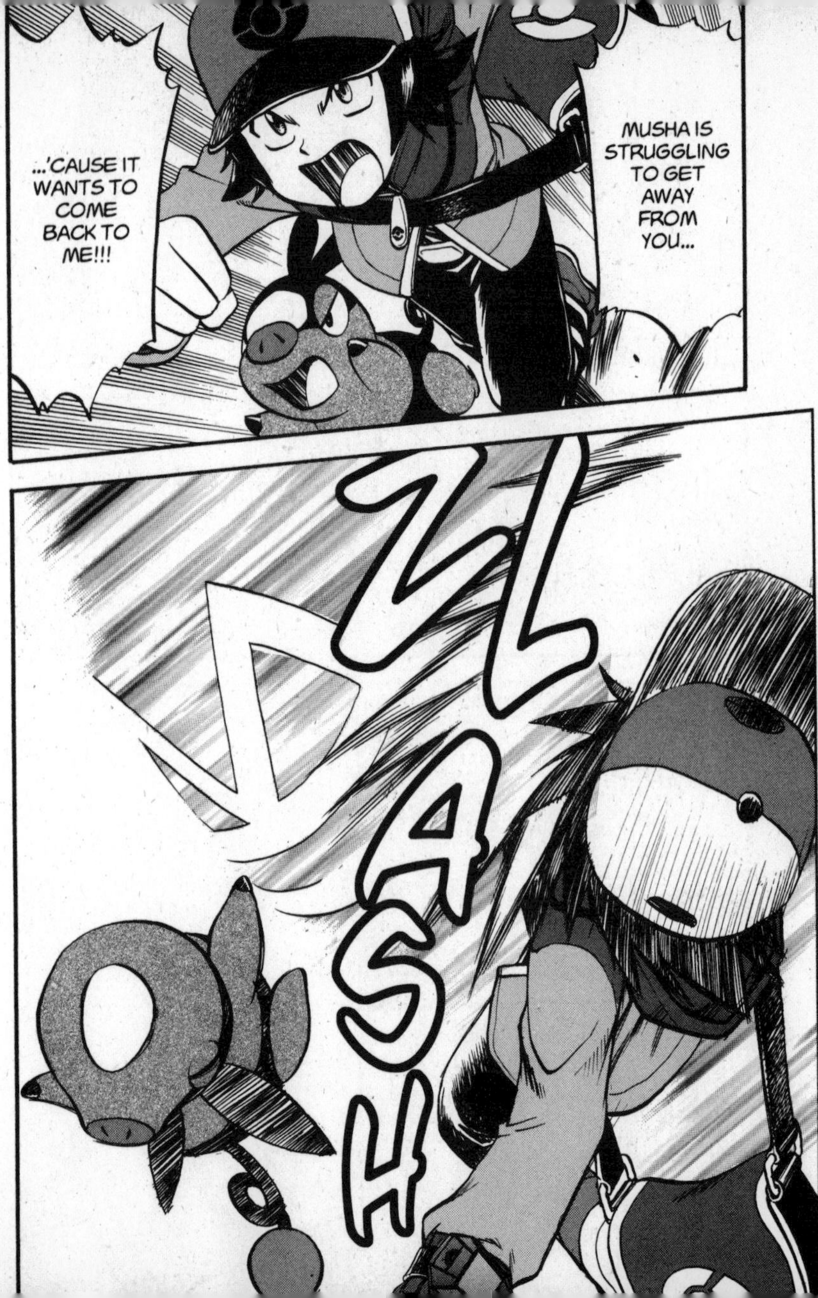
MUSHA IS STRUGGLING TO GET AWAY FROM YOU...
...'CAUSE IT WANTS TO COME BACK TO ME!!!

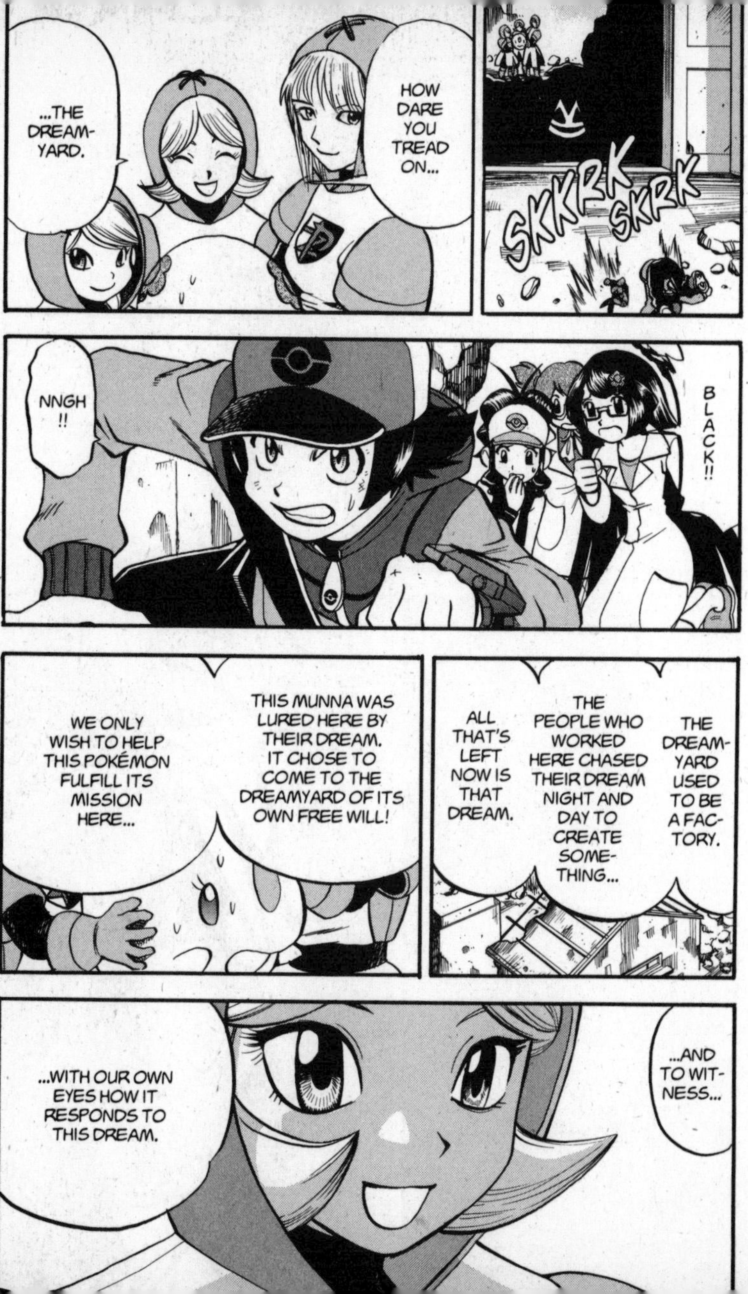
SKKRK SKRK
HOW DARE YOU TREAD ON...
...THE DREAM-YARD.
BLACK!!
NNGH!!
THE DREAM-YARD USED TO BE A FAC-TORY.
THE PEOPLE WHO WORKED HERE CHASED THEIR DREAM NIGHT AND DAY TO CREATE SOME-THING...
ALL THAT'S LEFT NOW IS THAT DREAM.
THIS MUNNA WAS LURED HERE BY THEIR DREAM. IT CHOSE TO COME TO THE DREAMYARD OF ITS OWN FREE WILL!
WE ONLY WISH TO HELP THIS POKÉMON FULFILL ITS MISSION HERE...
...AND TO WIT-NESS...
...WITH OUR OWN EYES HOW IT RESPONDS TO THIS DREAM.

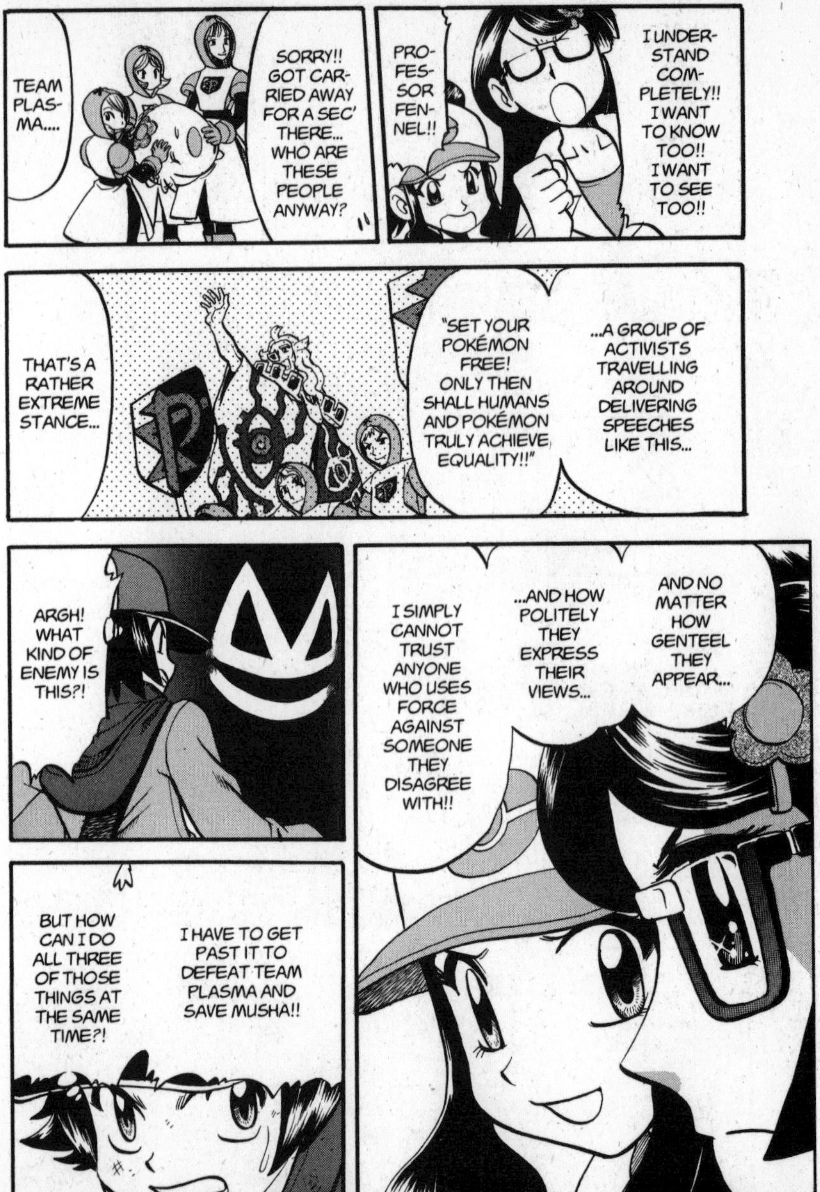
I UNDERSTAND COMPLETELY!! I WANT TO KNOW TOO!! I WANT TO SEE TOO!!
PROFESSOR FENNEL!!
SORRY!! GOT CARRIED AWAY FOR A SEC' THERE... WHO ARE THESE PEOPLE ANYWAY?
TEAM PLASMA....
...A GROUP OF ACTIVISTS TRAVELLING AROUND DELIVERING SPEECHES LIKE THIS...
"SET YOUR POKÉMON FREE! ONLY THEN SHALL HUMANS AND POKÉMON TRULY ACHIEVE EQUALITY!!"
THAT'S A RATHER EXTREME STANCE...
AND NO MATTER HOW GENTEEL THEY APPEAR...
...AND HOW POLITELY THEY EXPRESS THEIR VIEWS...
I SIMPLY CANNOT TRUST ANYONE WHO USES FORCE AGAINST SOMEONE THEY DISAGREE WITH!!
ARGH! WHAT KIND OF ENEMY IS THIS?!
I HAVE TO GET PAST IT TO DEFEAT TEAM PLASMA AND SAVE MUSHA!!
BUT HOW CAN I DO ALL THREE OF THOSE THINGS AT THE SAME TIME?!

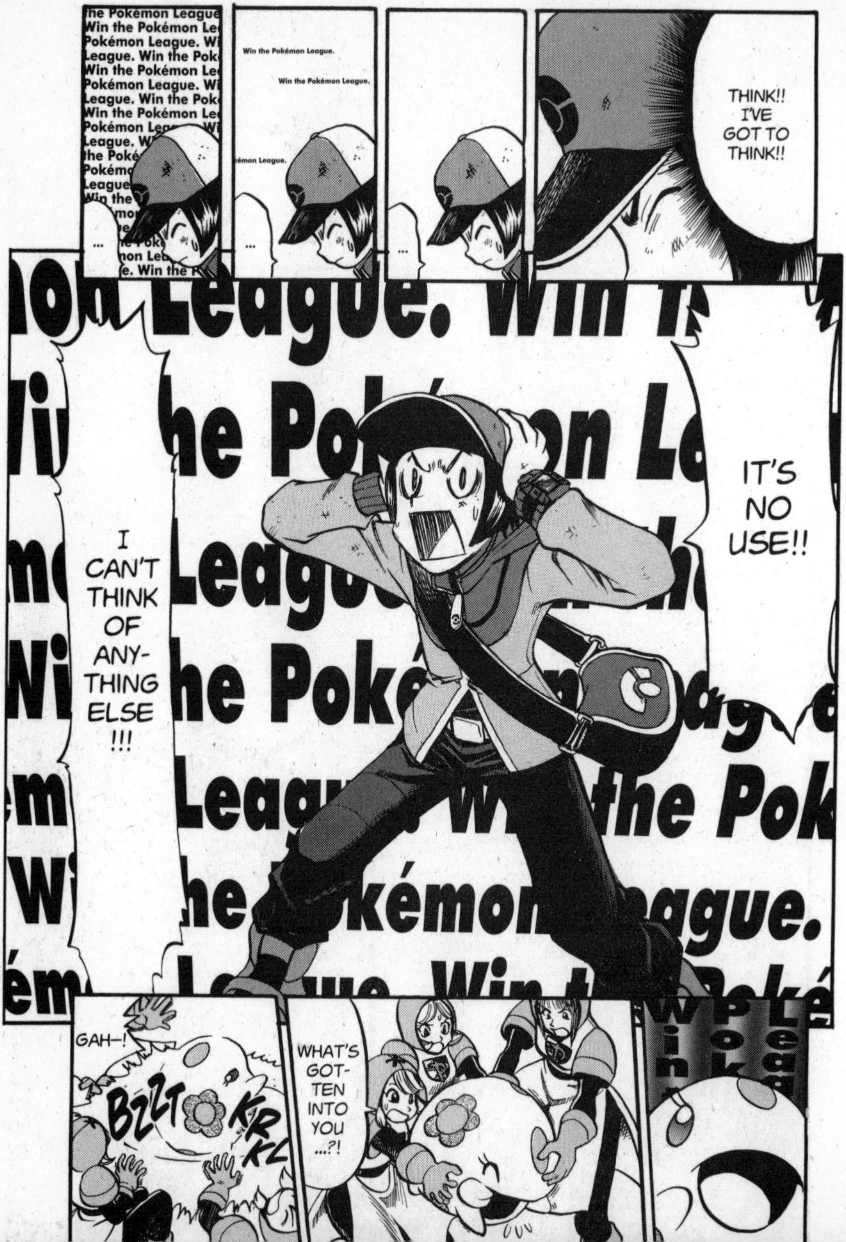
Win the Pokémon League.
...
Win the Pokémon League.
Win the Pokémon League.
...
...
THINK!! I'VE GOT TO THINK!!
I CAN'T THINK OF ANY-THING ELSE!!!
IT'S NO USE!!
GAH-!
BZZT
KRKL
WHAT'S GOT-TEN INTO YOU...?!

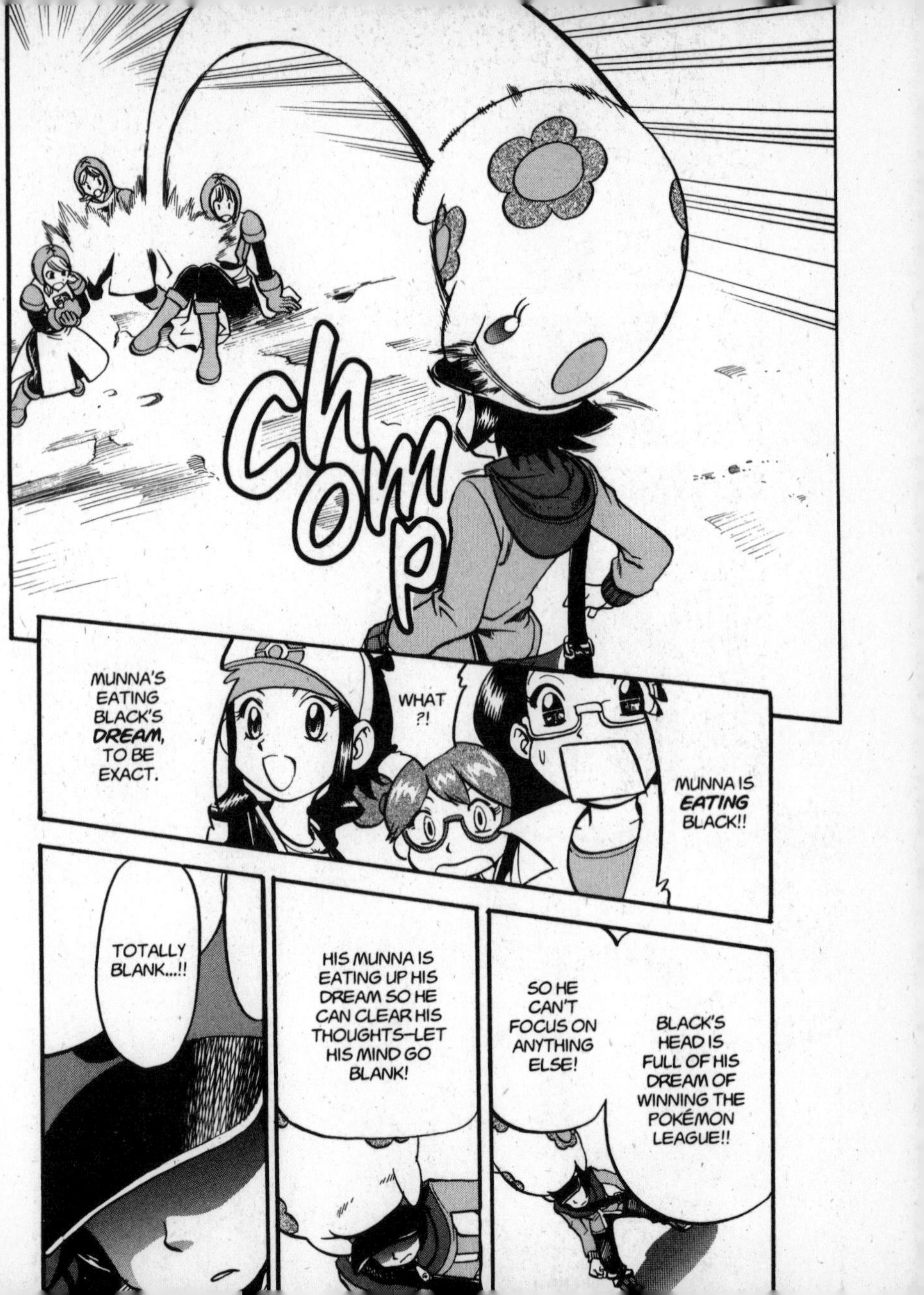
Chomp
MUNNA IS EATING BLACK!!
WHAT?!
MUNNA'S EATING BLACK'S DREAM, TO BE EXACT.
BLACK'S HEAD IS FULL OF HIS DREAM OF WINNING THE POKÉMON LEAGUE!!
SO HE CAN'T FOCUS ON ANYTHING ELSE!
HIS MUNNA IS EATING UP HIS DREAM SO HE CAN CLEAR HIS THOUGHTS—LET HIS MIND GO BLANK!
TOTALLY BLANK...!!

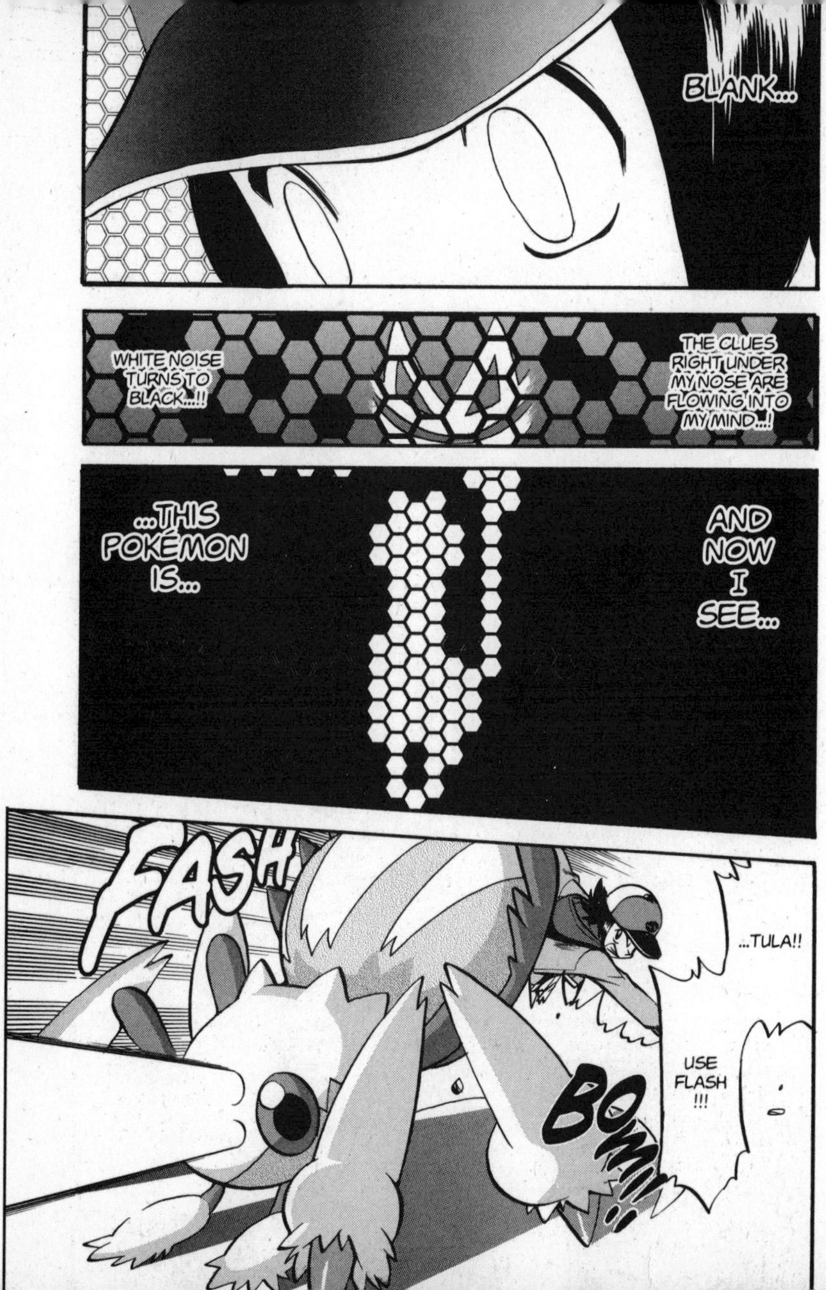
BLANK...
THE CLUES RIGHT UNDER MY NOSE ARE FLOWING INTO MY MIND...!
WHITE NOISE TURNS TO BLACK...!!
AND NOW I SEE...
...THIS POKÉMON IS...
...TULA!!
USE FLASH!!!
BOMM!!
FASH

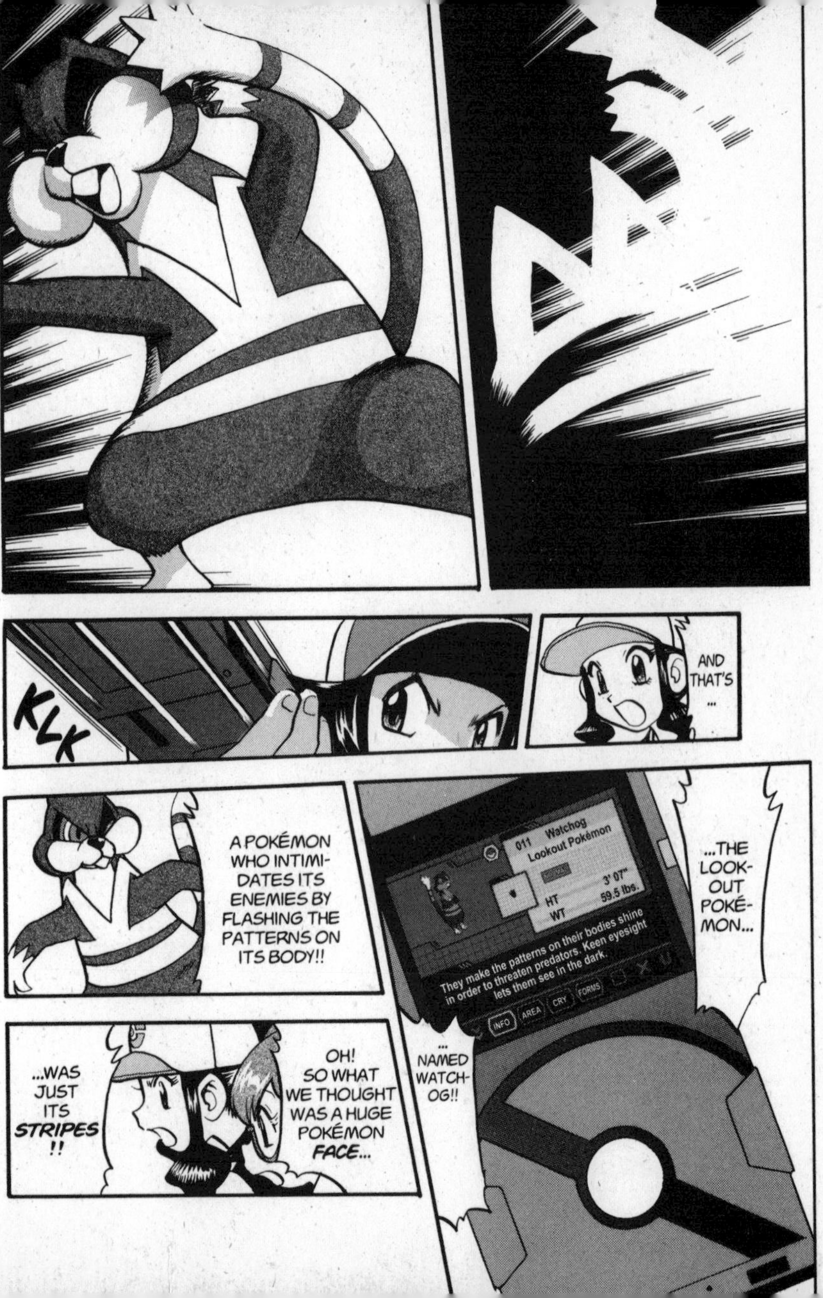
KLK
AND THAT'S...
A POKÉMON WHO INTIMIDATES ITS ENEMIES BY FLASHING THE PATTERNS ON ITS BODY!!
...THE LOOKOUT POKÉMON...
011 Watchog
Lookout Pokémon
HT 3' 07"
WT 59.5 lbs.
They make the patterns on their bodies shine in order to threaten predators. Keen eyesight lets them see in the dark.
INFO
AREA
CRY
FORMS
...NAMED WATCHOG!!
OH! SO WHAT WE THOUGHT WAS A HUGE POKÉMON FACE...
...WAS JUST ITS STRIPES!!

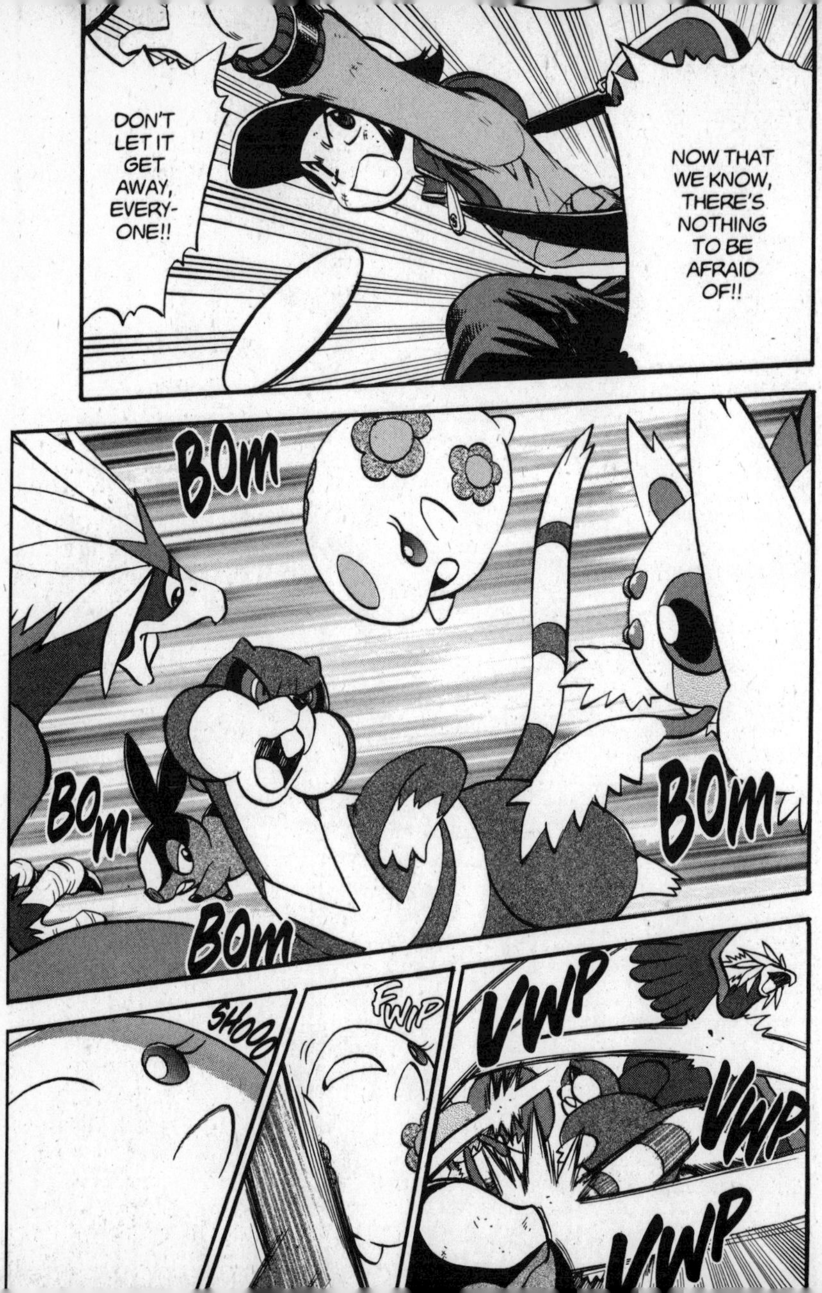
NOW THAT WE KNOW, THERE'S NOTHING TO BE AFRAID OF!!
DON'T LET IT GET AWAY, EVERY-ONE!!
BOM
BOM
BOM
BOM
VWP
FWIP
SHOOO
VWP
VWP

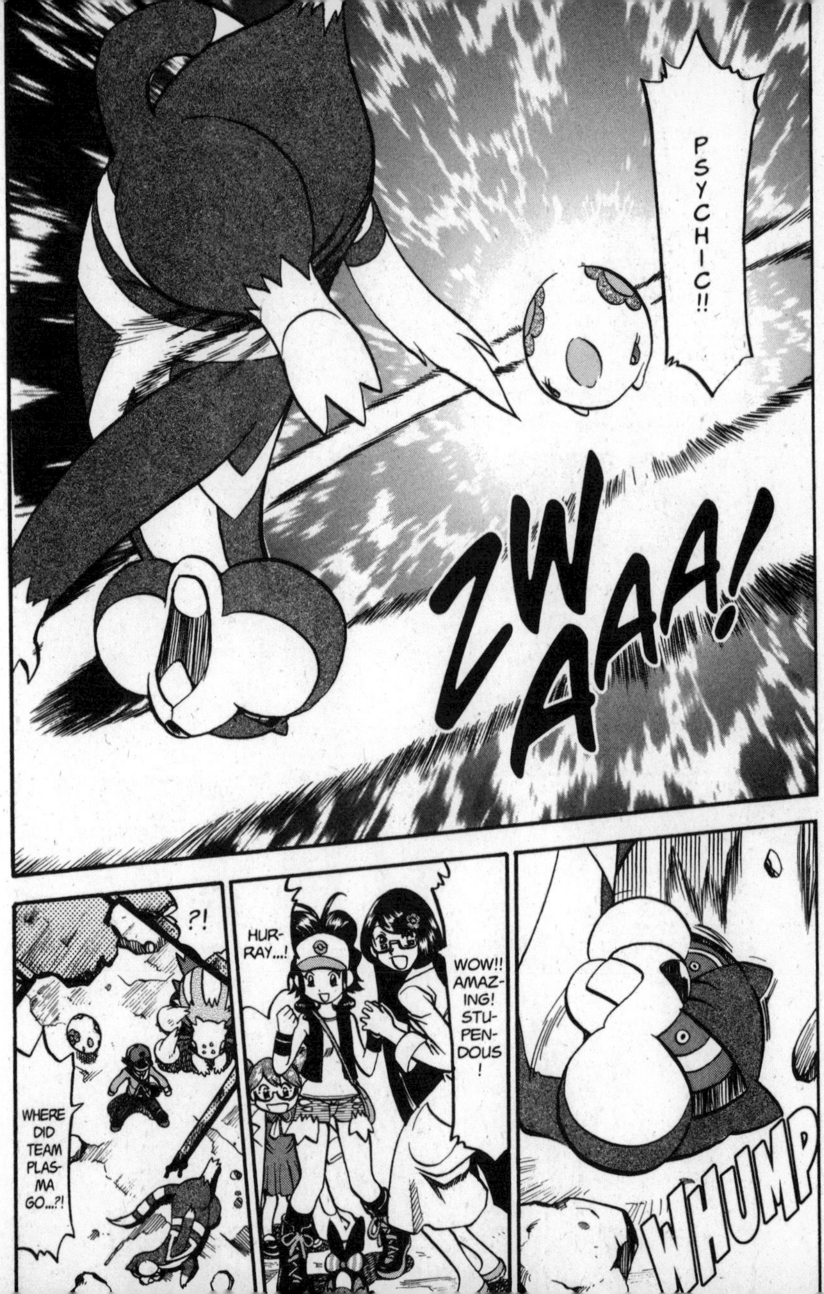
PSYCHIC!!
ZWAAAA!
WHUMP
WOW!! AMAZ-ING! STU-PEN-DOUS!
HUR-RAY...!
?!
WHERE DID TEAM PLAS-MA GO...?!

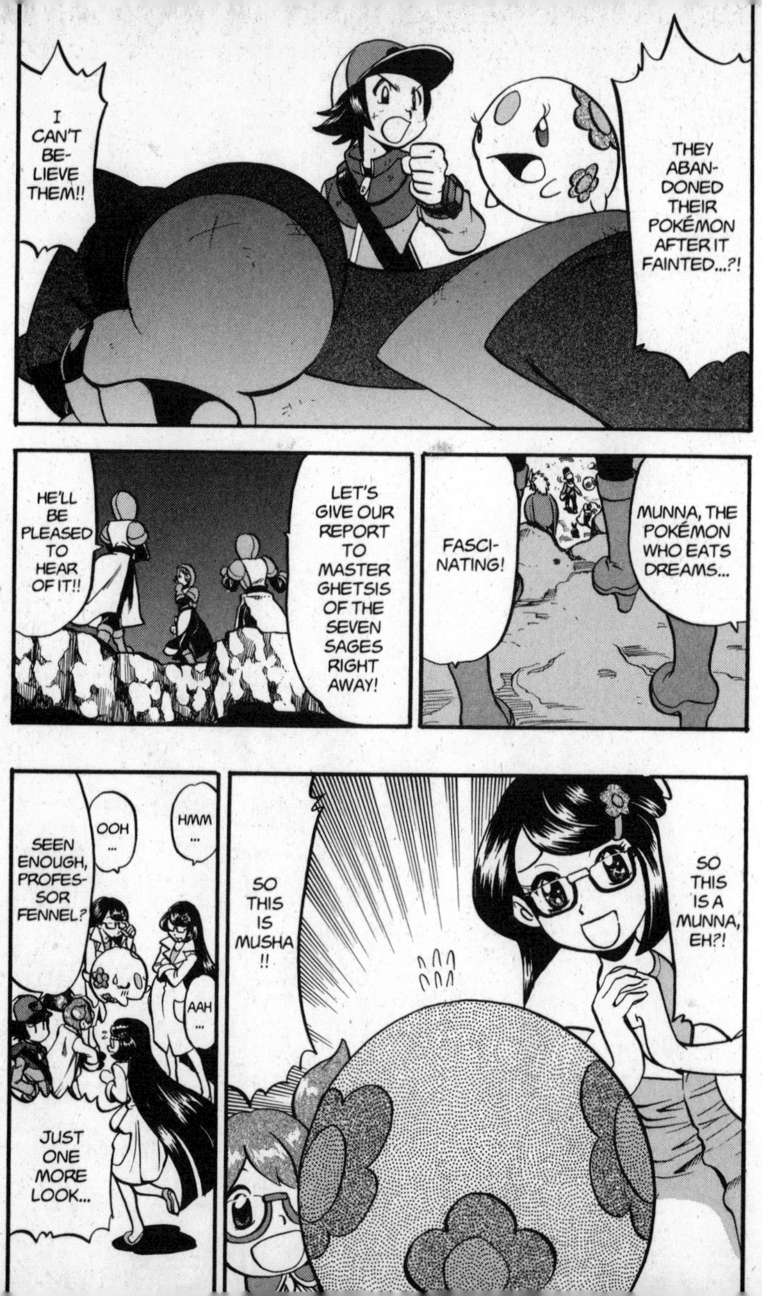
THEY ABANDONED THEIR POKÉMON AFTER IT FAINTED...?!
I CAN'T BELIEVE THEM!!
MUNNA, THE POKÉMON WHO EATS DREAMS...
FASCINATING!
LET'S GIVE OUR REPORT TO MASTER GHETSIS OF THE SEVEN SAGES RIGHT AWAY!
HE'LL BE PLEASED TO HEAR OF IT!!
SO THIS IS A MUNNA, EH?!
SO THIS IS MUSHA!!
HMM...
OOH...
SEEN ENOUGH, PROFESSOR FENNEL?
AAH...
JUST ONE MORE LOOK...

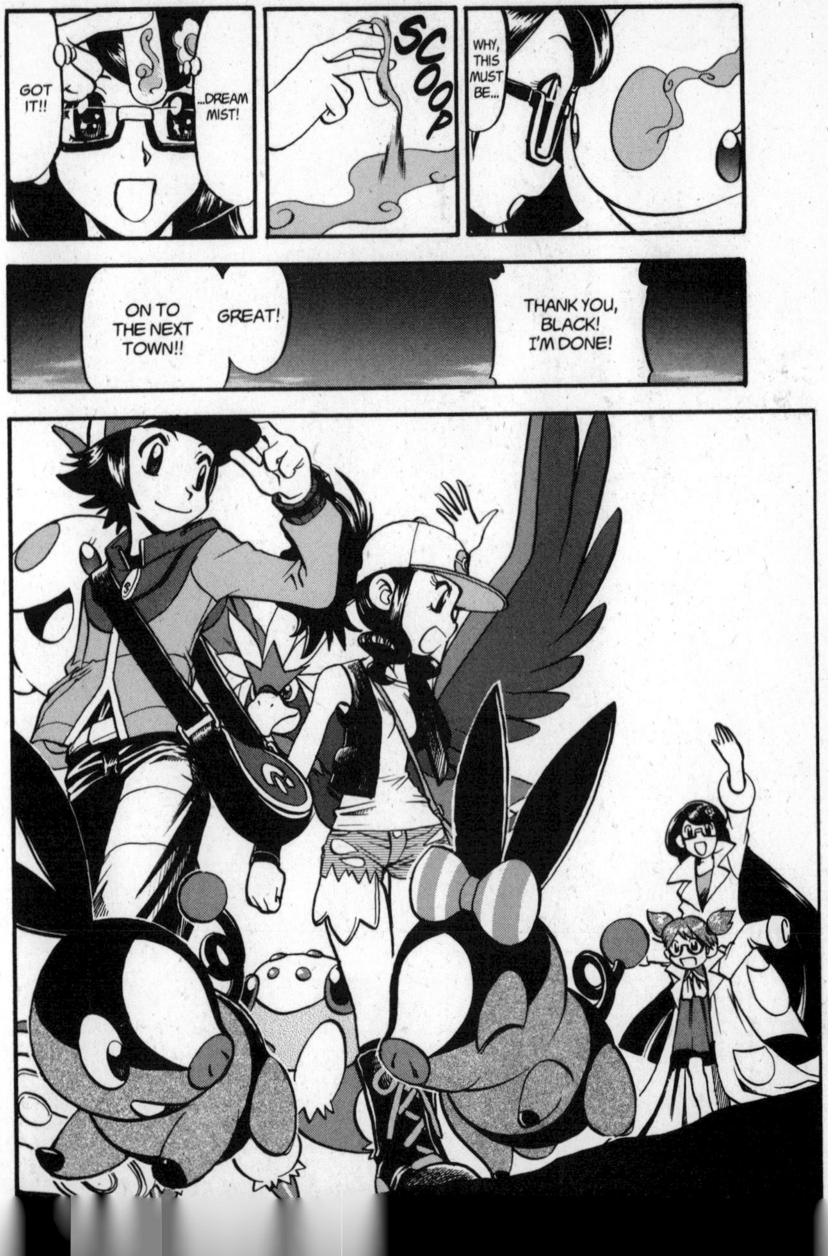
WHY, THIS MUST BE...
SCOOP
...DREAM MIST!
GOT IT!!
THANK YOU, BLACK! I'M DONE!
GREAT!
ON TO THE NEXT TOWN!!

Adventure ⑫
Wheeling and Dealing

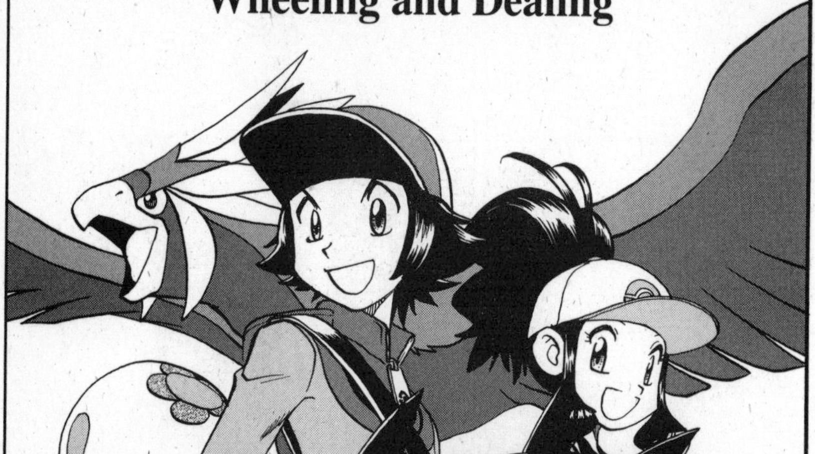

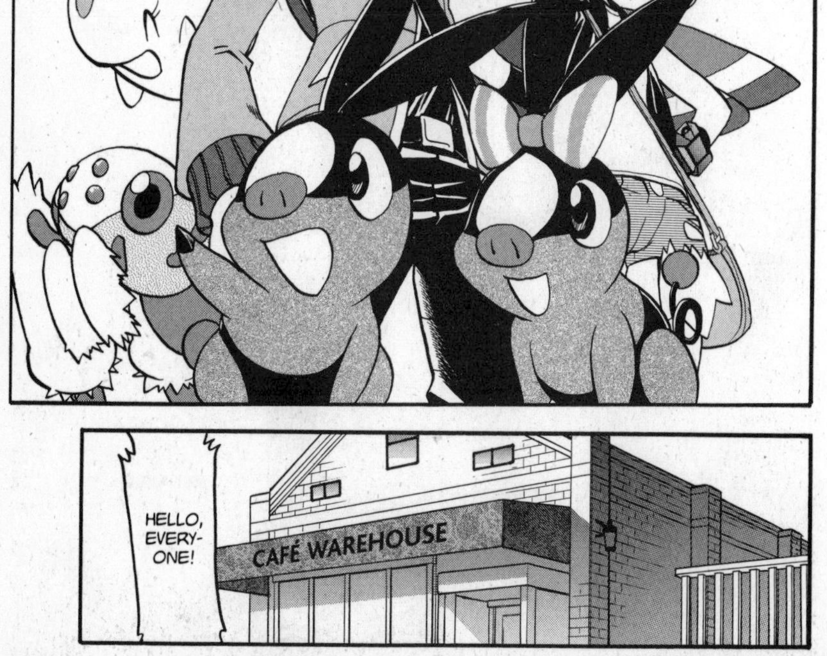
HELLO, EVERY-ONE!
CAFÉ WAREHOUSE

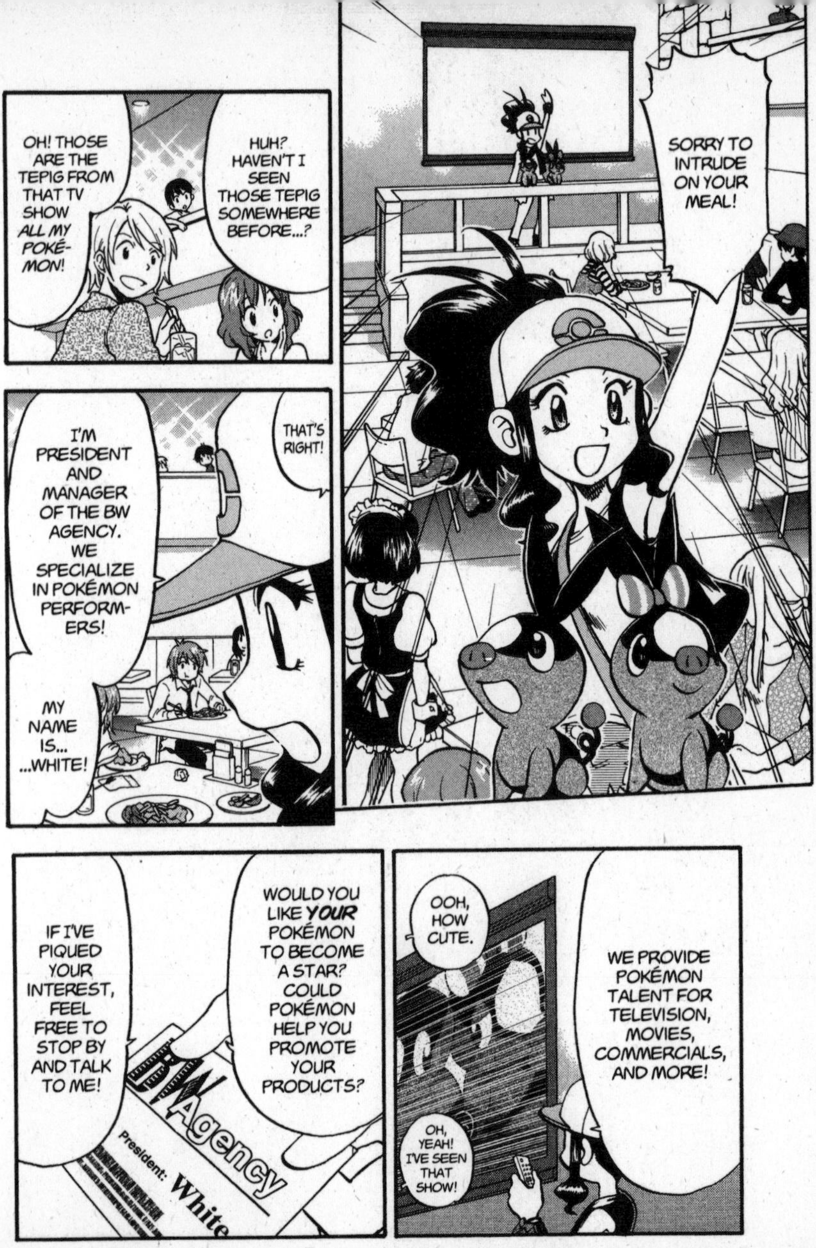
SORRY TO INTRUDE ON YOUR MEAL!
HUH? HAVEN'T I SEEN THOSE TEPIG SOMEWHERE BEFORE...?
OH! THOSE ARE THE TEPIG FROM THAT TV SHOW *ALL MY POKÉMON*!
THAT'S RIGHT!
I'M PRESIDENT AND MANAGER OF THE BW AGENCY. WE SPECIALIZE IN POKÉMON PERFORMERS!
MY NAME IS... ...WHITE!
WE PROVIDE POKÉMON TALENT FOR TELEVISION, MOVIES, COMMERCIALS, AND MORE!
OOH, HOW CUTE.
OH, YEAH! I'VE SEEN THAT SHOW!
WOULD YOU LIKE ***YOUR*** POKÉMON TO BECOME A STAR? COULD POKÉMON HELP YOU PROMOTE YOUR PRODUCTS?
IF I'VE PIQUED YOUR INTEREST, FEEL FREE TO STOP BY AND TALK TO ME!
BW Agency
President: White

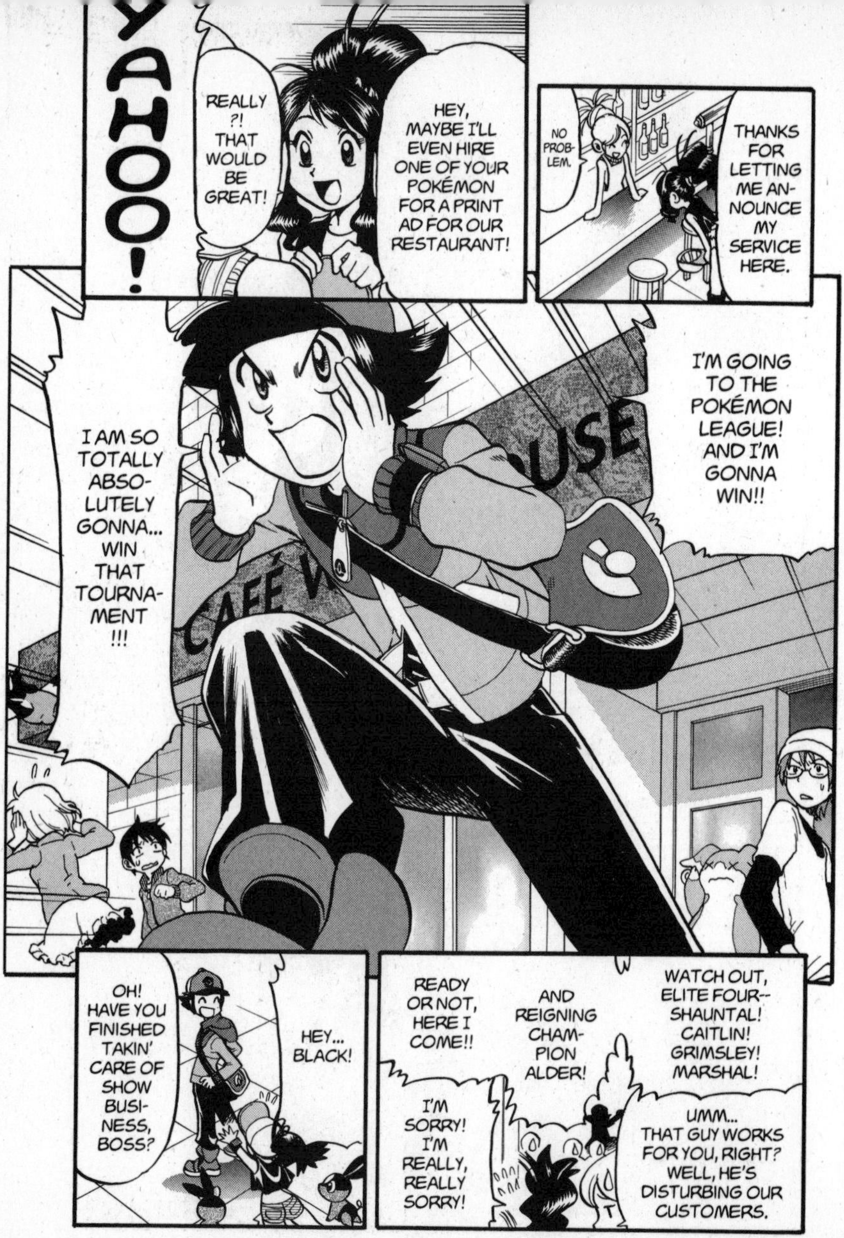
THANKS FOR LETTING ME ANNOUNCE MY SERVICE HERE.
NO PROBLEM.
HEY, MAYBE I'LL EVEN HIRE ONE OF YOUR POKÉMON FOR A PRINT AD FOR OUR RESTAURANT!
REALLY ?! THAT WOULD BE GREAT!
YAHOO!
I'M GOING TO THE POKÉMON LEAGUE! AND I'M GONNA WIN!!
I AM SO TOTALLY ABSOLUTELY GONNA... WIN THAT TOURNAMENT !!!
USE
CAFÉ
WATCH OUT, ELITE FOUR-- SHAUNTAL! CAITLIN! GRIMSLEY! MARSHAL!
AND REIGNING CHAMPION ALDER!
READY OR NOT, HERE I COME!!
UMM... THAT GUY WORKS FOR YOU, RIGHT? WELL, HE'S DISTURBING OUR CUSTOMERS.
I'M SORRY! I'M REALLY, REALLY SORRY!
HEY... BLACK!
OH! HAVE YOU FINISHED TAKIN' CARE OF SHOW BUSINESS, BOSS?

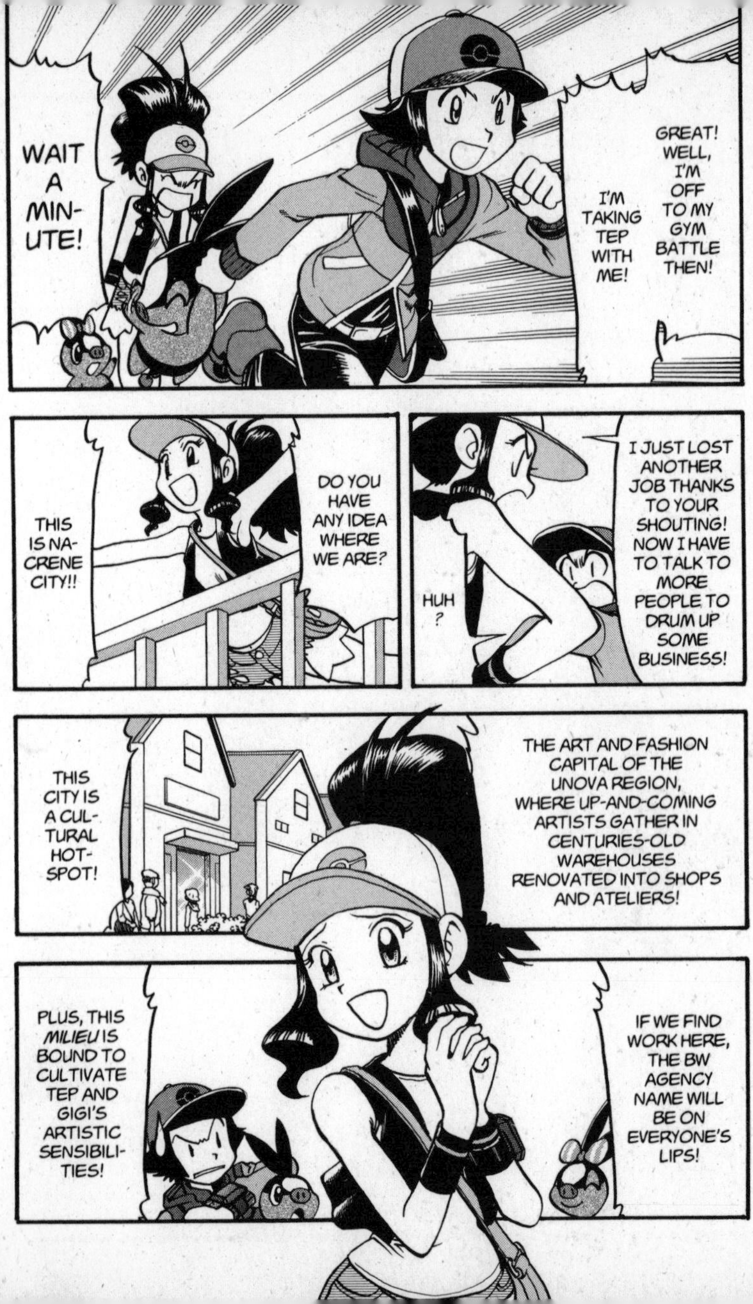
GREAT! WELL, I'M OFF TO MY GYM BATTLE THEN!
I'M TAKING TEP WITH ME!
WAIT A MIN-UTE!
DO YOU HAVE ANY IDEA WHERE WE ARE?
THIS IS NA-CRENE CITY!!
I JUST LOST ANOTHER JOB THANKS TO YOUR SHOUTING! NOW I HAVE TO TALK TO MORE PEOPLE TO DRUM UP SOME BUSINESS!
HUH ?
THE ART AND FASHION CAPITAL OF THE UNOVA REGION, WHERE UP-AND-COMING ARTISTS GATHER IN CENTURIES-OLD WAREHOUSES RENOVATED INTO SHOPS AND ATELIERS!
THIS CITY IS A CUL-TURAL HOT-SPOT!
IF WE FIND WORK HERE, THE BW AGENCY NAME WILL BE ON EVERYONE'S LIPS!
PLUS, THIS *MILIEU* IS BOUND TO CULTIVATE TEP AND GIGI'S ARTISTIC SENSIBILI-TIES!

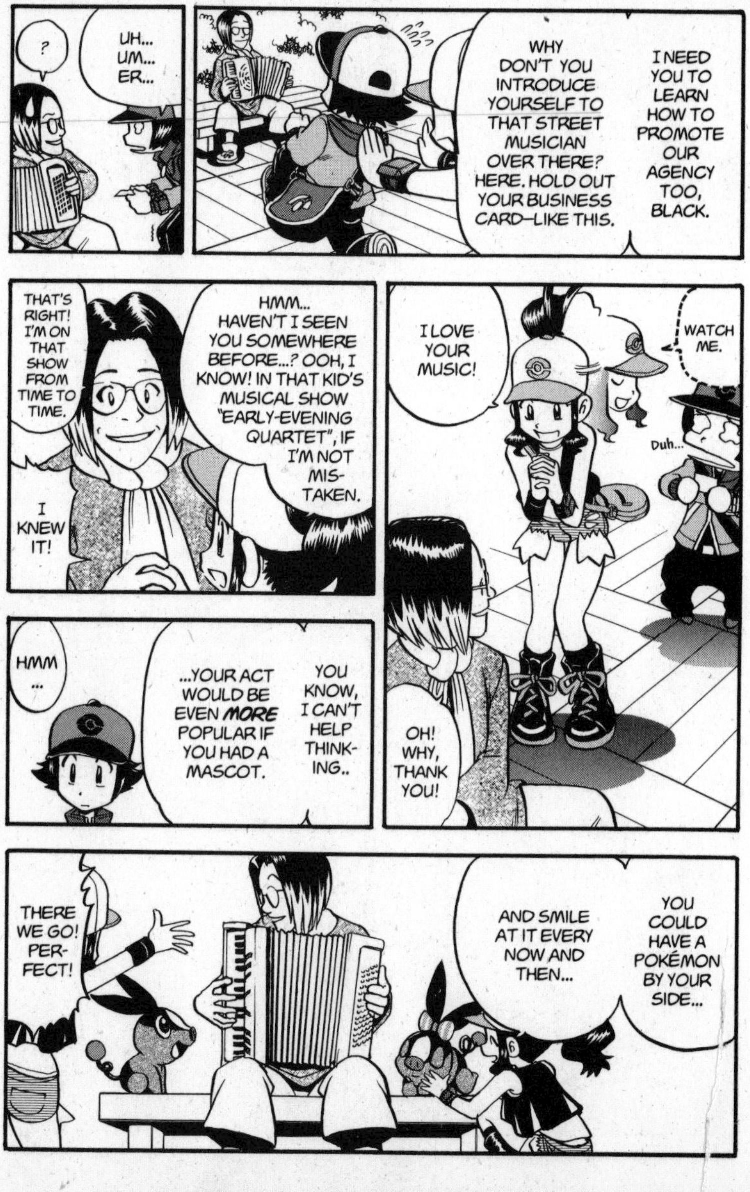
I NEED YOU TO LEARN HOW TO PROMOTE OUR AGENCY TOO, BLACK.
WHY DON'T YOU INTRODUCE YOURSELF TO THAT STREET MUSICIAN OVER THERE? HERE. HOLD OUT YOUR BUSINESS CARD—LIKE THIS.
UH... UM... ER...
?
WATCH ME.
I LOVE YOUR MUSIC!
Duh...
OH! WHY, THANK YOU!
HMM... HAVEN'T I SEEN YOU SOMEWHERE BEFORE...? OOH, I KNOW! IN THAT KID'S MUSICAL SHOW "EARLY-EVENING QUARTET", IF I'M NOT MIS-TAKEN.
THAT'S RIGHT! I'M ON THAT SHOW FROM TIME TO TIME.
I KNEW IT!
YOU KNOW, I CAN'T HELP THINK-ING..
...YOUR ACT WOULD BE EVEN ***MORE*** POPULAR IF YOU HAD A MASCOT.
HMM ...
YOU COULD HAVE A POKÉMON BY YOUR SIDE...
AND SMILE AT IT EVERY NOW AND THEN...
THERE WE GO! PER-FECT!

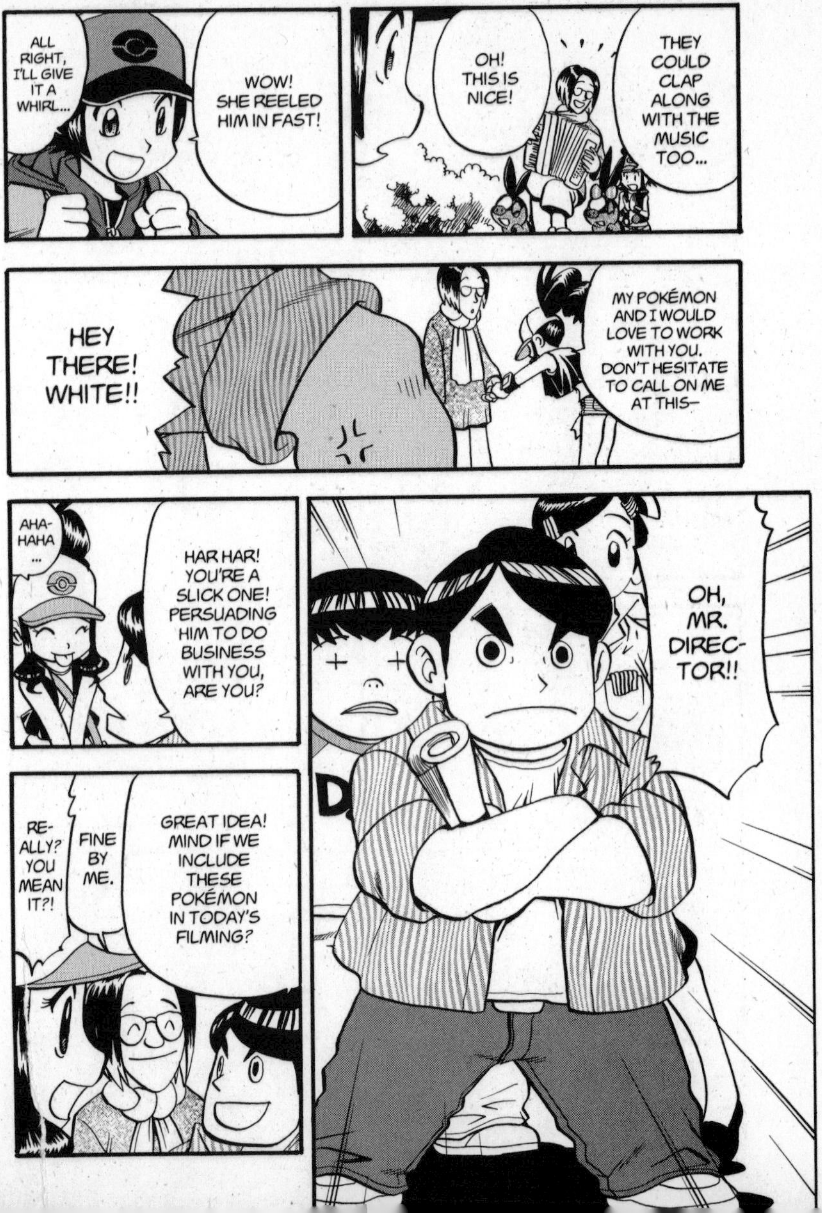
ALL RIGHT, I'LL GIVE IT A WHIRL...
WOW! SHE REELED HIM IN FAST!
OH! THIS IS NICE!
THEY COULD CLAP ALONG WITH THE MUSIC TOO...
MY POKÉMON AND I WOULD LOVE TO WORK WITH YOU. DON'T HESITATE TO CALL ON ME AT THIS—
HEY THERE! WHITE!!
AHA-HAHA ...
HAR HAR! YOU'RE A SLICK ONE! PERSUADING HIM TO DO BUSINESS WITH YOU, ARE YOU?
OH, MR. DIREC-TOR!!
GREAT IDEA! MIND IF WE INCLUDE THESE POKÉMON IN TODAY'S FILMING?
FINE BY ME.
RE-ALLY? YOU MEAN IT?!

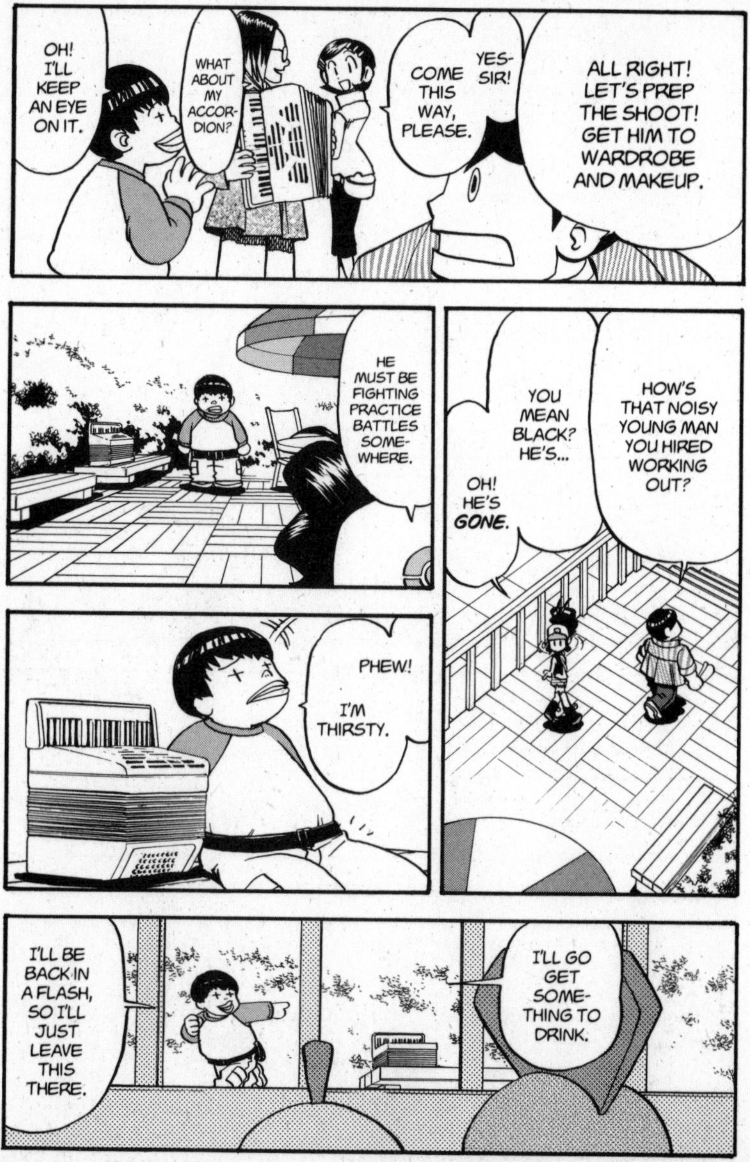
ALL RIGHT! LET'S PREP THE SHOOT! GET HIM TO WARDROBE AND MAKEUP.
YES-SIR!
COME THIS WAY, PLEASE.
WHAT ABOUT MY ACCORDION?
OH! I'LL KEEP AN EYE ON IT.
HOW'S THAT NOISY YOUNG MAN YOU HIRED WORKING OUT?
YOU MEAN BLACK? HE'S...
OH! HE'S *GONE*.
HE MUST BE FIGHTING PRACTICE BATTLES SOME-WHERE.
PHEW!
I'M THIRSTY.
I'LL GO GET SOME-THING TO DRINK.
I'LL BE BACK IN A FLASH, SO I'LL JUST LEAVE THIS THERE.

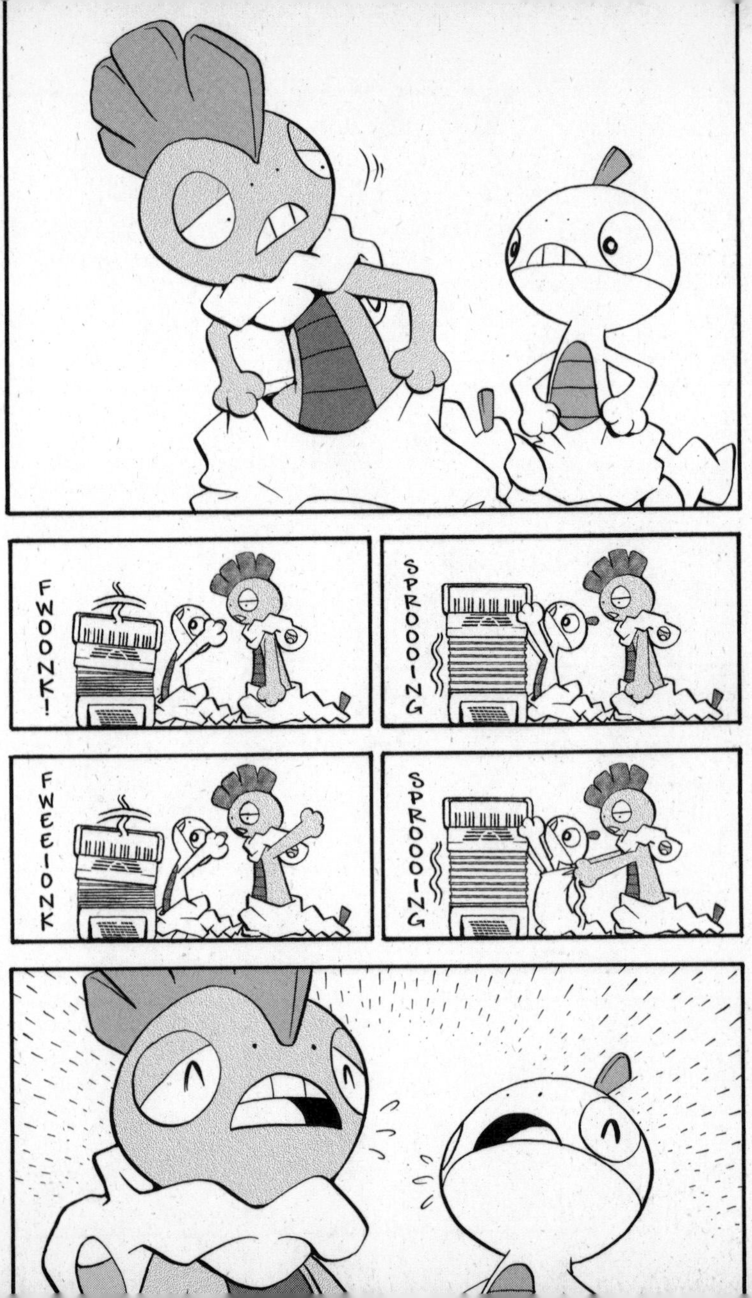
SPROOOOING
FWOONK!
SPROOOOING
FWEEIONK

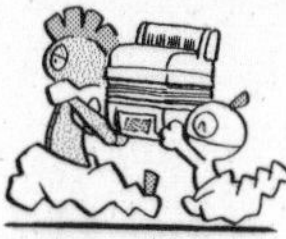

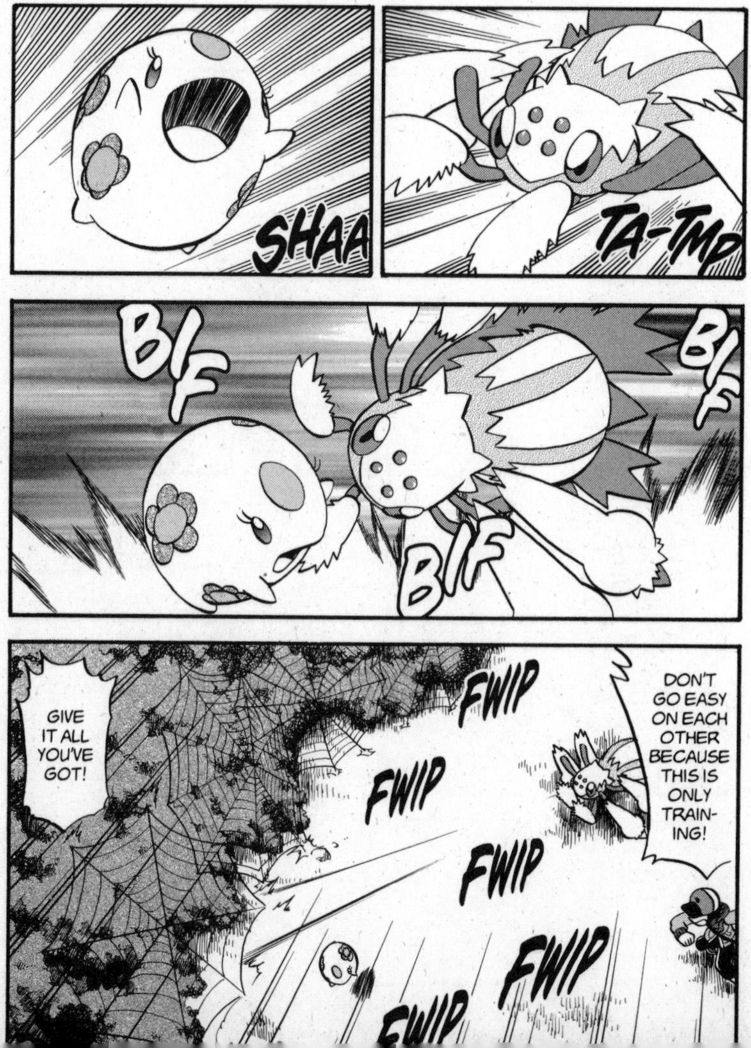
SHAA
TA-TMP
BIF
BIF
BIF
GIVE IT ALL YOU'VE GOT!
DON'T GO EASY ON EACH OTHER BECAUSE THIS IS ONLY TRAIN-ING!
FWIP
FWIP
FWIP
FWIP
FWIP

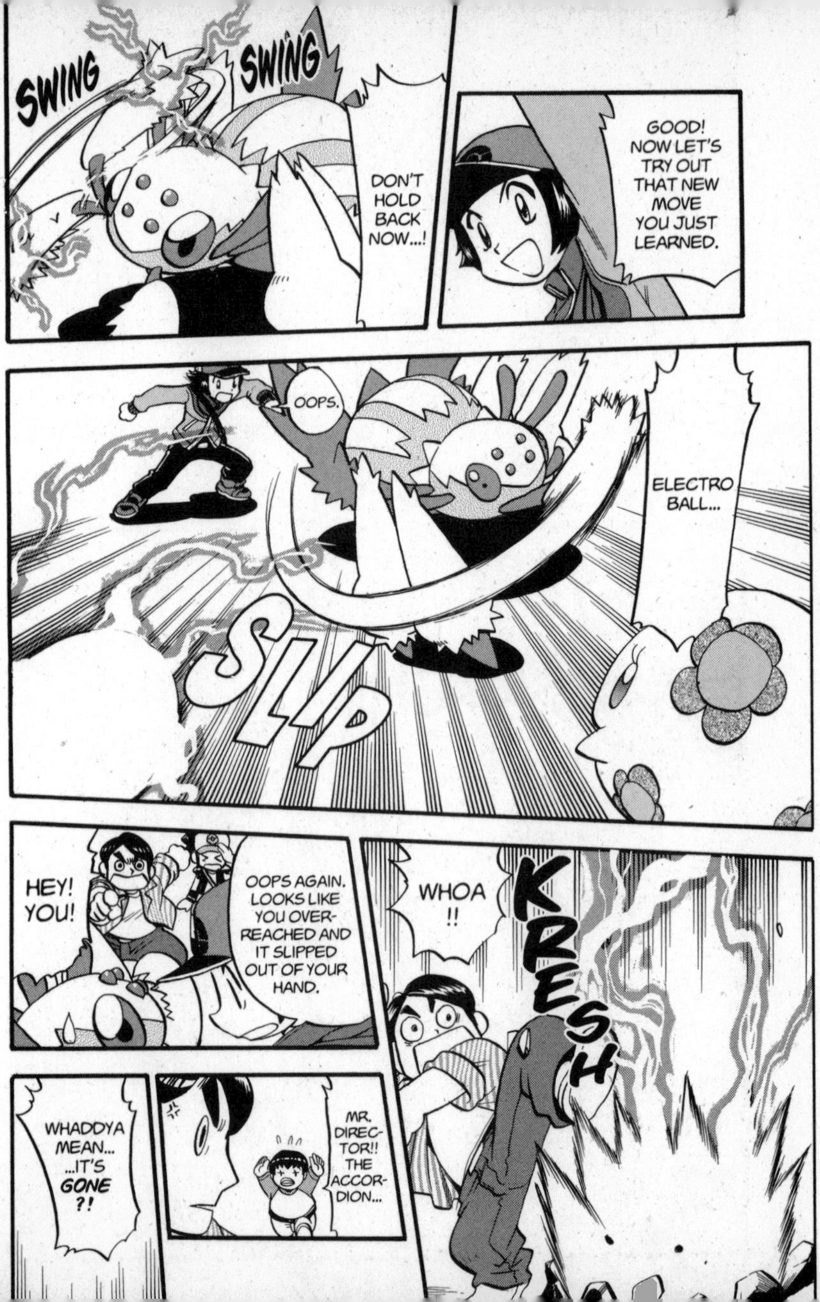
SWING
SWING
DON'T HOLD BACK NOW...!
GOOD! NOW LET'S TRY OUT THAT NEW MOVE YOU JUST LEARNED.
OOPS.
ELECTRO BALL...
SLIP
HEY! YOU!
OOPS AGAIN. LOOKS LIKE YOU OVER-REACHED AND IT SLIPPED OUT OF YOUR HAND.
WHOA!!
KRESH
WHADDYA MEAN... ...IT'S GONE?!
MR. DIRECTOR!! THE ACCORDION...

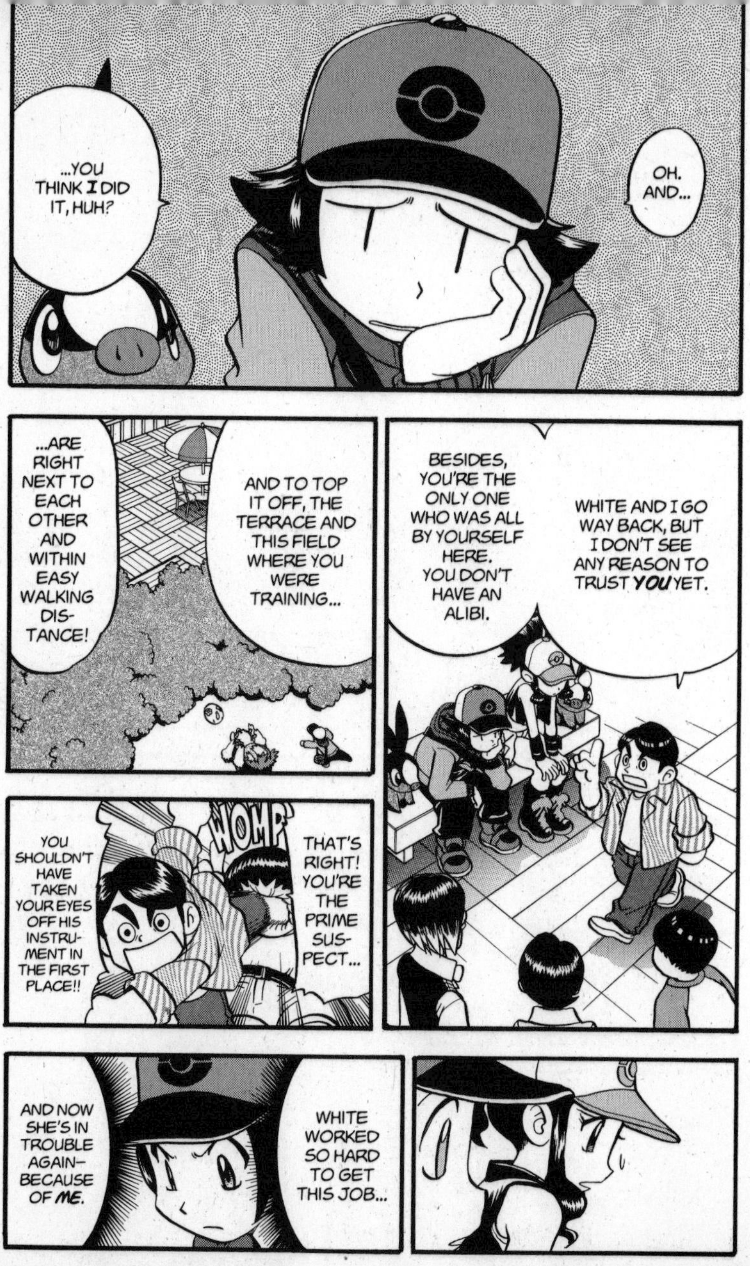
OH. AND...
...YOU THINK I DID IT, HUH?
WHITE AND I GO WAY BACK, BUT I DON'T SEE ANY REASON TO TRUST YOU YET.
BESIDES, YOU'RE THE ONLY ONE WHO WAS ALL BY YOURSELF HERE. YOU DON'T HAVE AN ALIBI.
AND TO TOP IT OFF, THE TERRACE AND THIS FIELD WHERE YOU WERE TRAINING...
...ARE RIGHT NEXT TO EACH OTHER AND WITHIN EASY WALKING DIS-TANCE!
THAT'S RIGHT! YOU'RE THE PRIME SUS-PECT...
WOMP
YOU SHOULDN'T HAVE TAKEN YOUR EYES OFF HIS INSTRU-MENT IN THE FIRST PLACE!!
WHITE WORKED SO HARD TO GET THIS JOB...
AND NOW SHE'S IN TROUBLE AGAIN—BECAUSE OF ME.

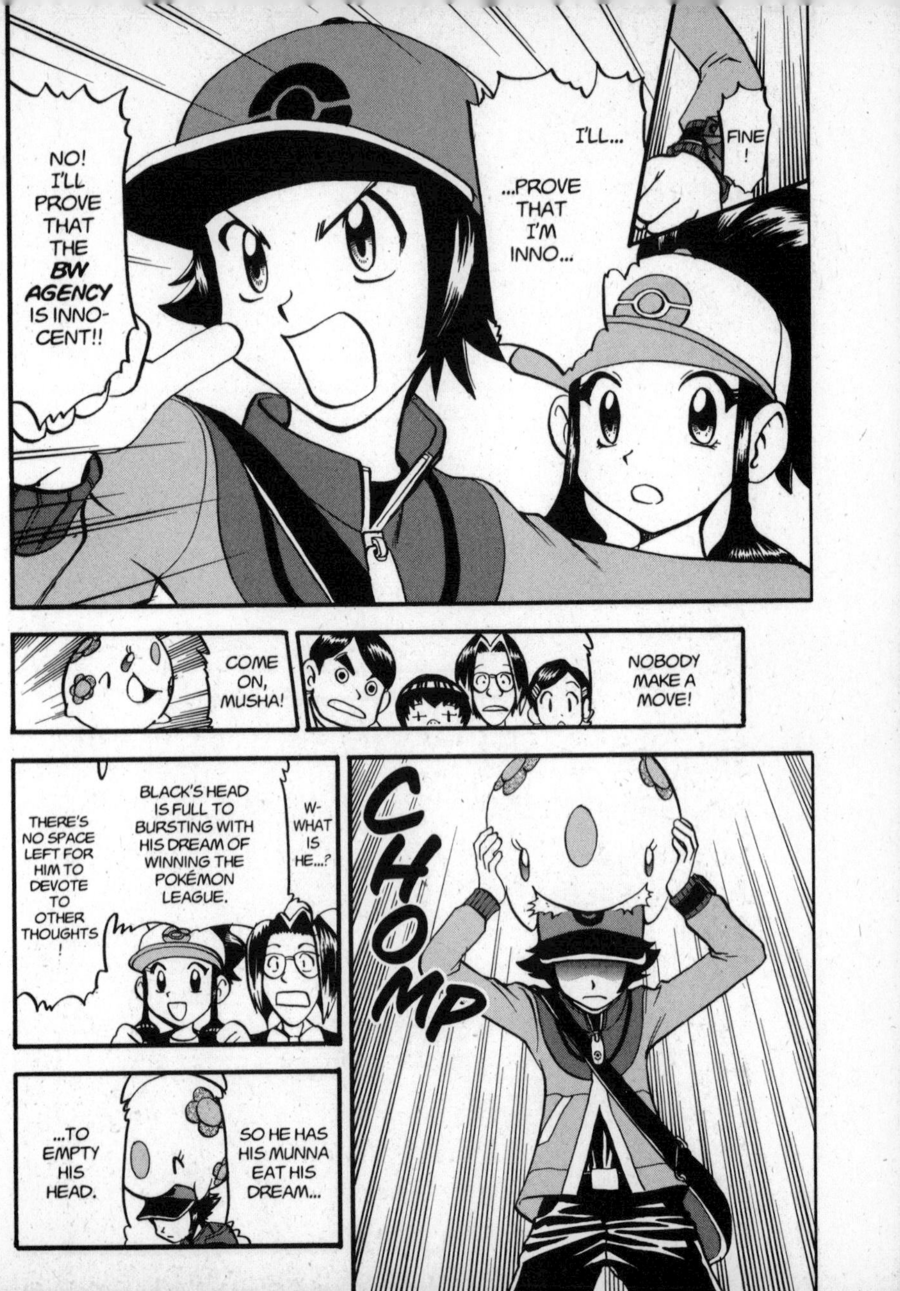
FINE!
I'LL...
...PROVE THAT I'M INNO...
NO! I'LL PROVE THAT THE BW AGENCY IS INNOCENT!!
COME ON, MUSHA!
NOBODY MAKE A MOVE!
THERE'S NO SPACE LEFT FOR HIM TO DEVOTE TO OTHER THOUGHTS!
BLACK'S HEAD IS FULL TO BURSTING WITH HIS DREAM OF WINNING THE POKÉMON LEAGUE.
W-WHAT IS HE...?
CHOMP
...TO EMPTY HIS HEAD.
SO HE HAS HIS MUNNA EAT HIS DREAM...

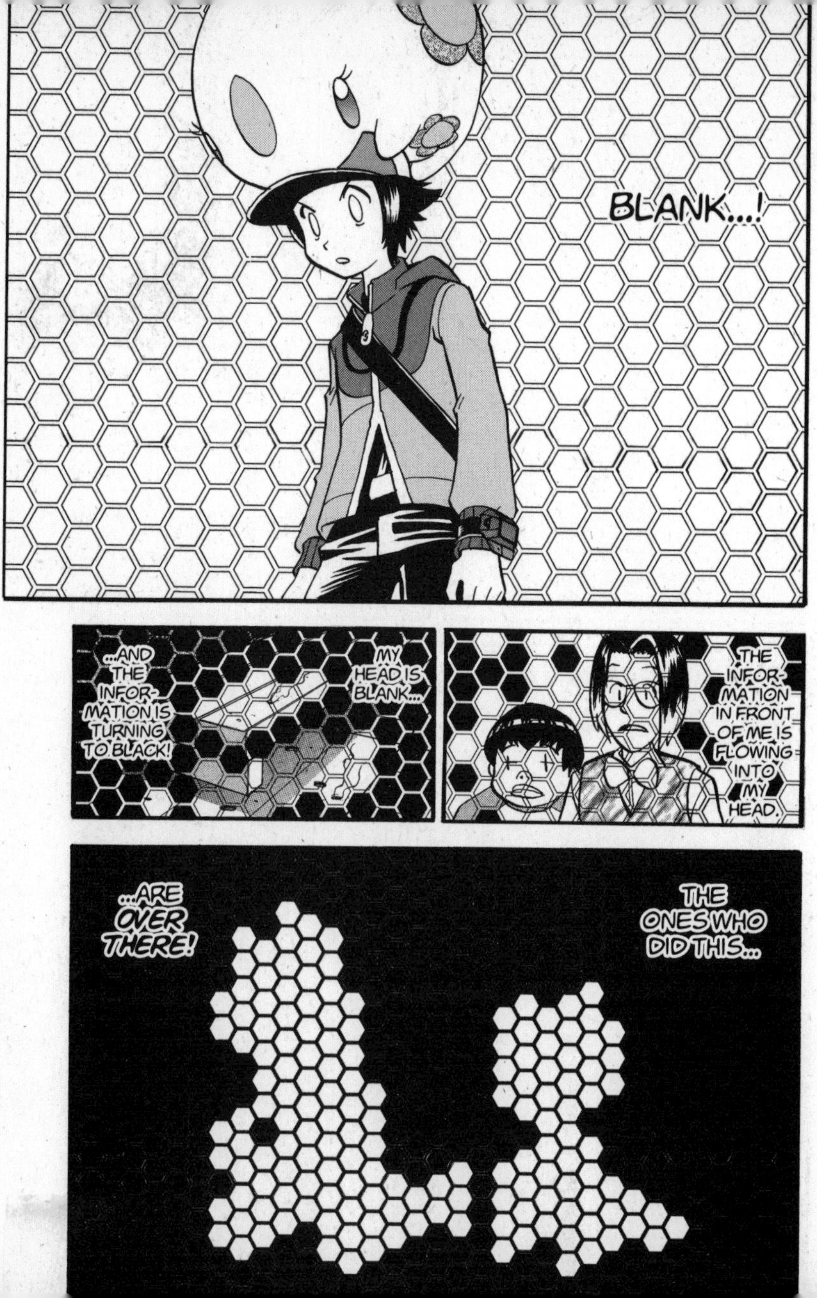
BLANK...!
MY HEAD IS BLANK...
...AND THE INFORMATION IS TURNING TO BLACK!
THE INFORMATION IN FRONT OF ME IS FLOWING INTO MY HEAD.
THE ONES WHO DID THIS...
...ARE OVER THERE!

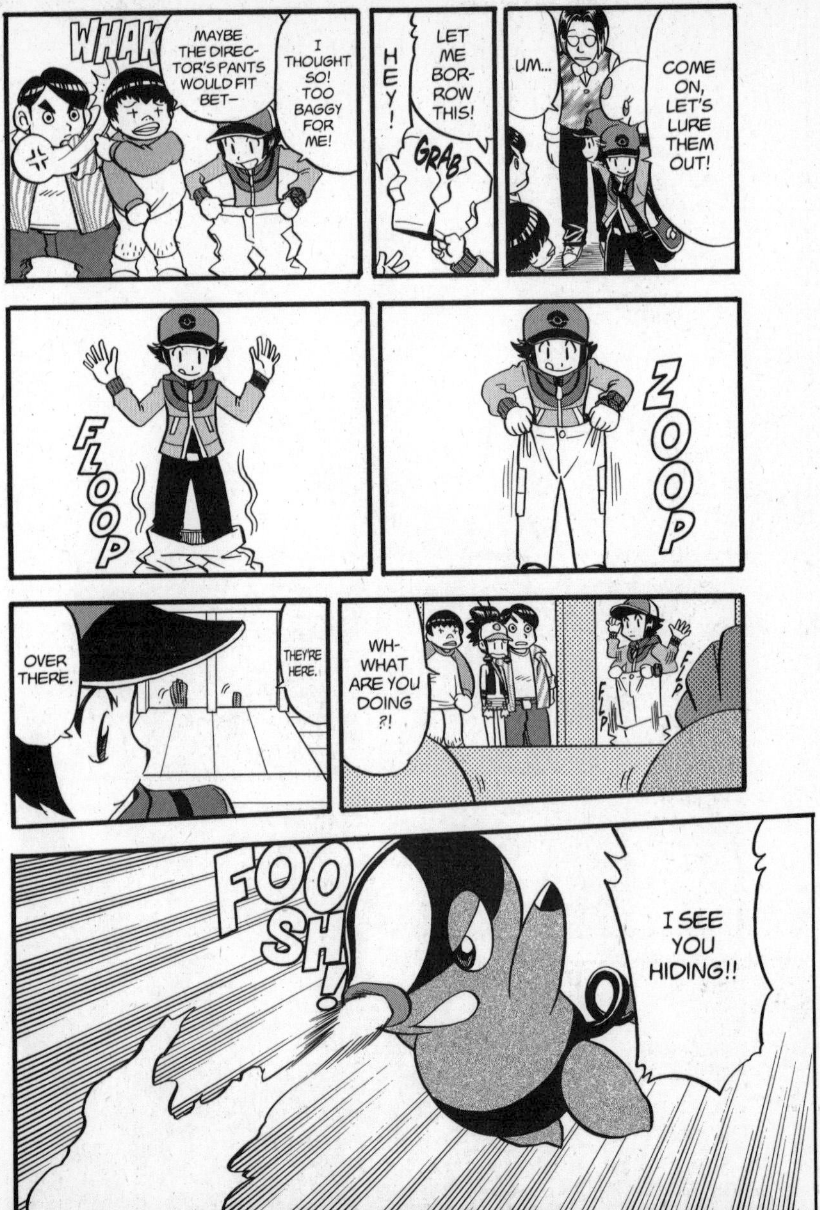
WHAK
MAYBE THE DIRECTOR'S PANTS WOULD FIT BET–
I THOUGHT SO! TOO BAGGY FOR ME!
HEY!
LET ME BORROW THIS!
GRAB
UM...
COME ON, LET'S LURE THEM OUT!
FLOOP
ZOOP
OVER THERE.
THEY'RE HERE.
WH-WHAT ARE YOU DOING ?!
FLP FLP
FOOSH!
I SEE YOU HIDING!!

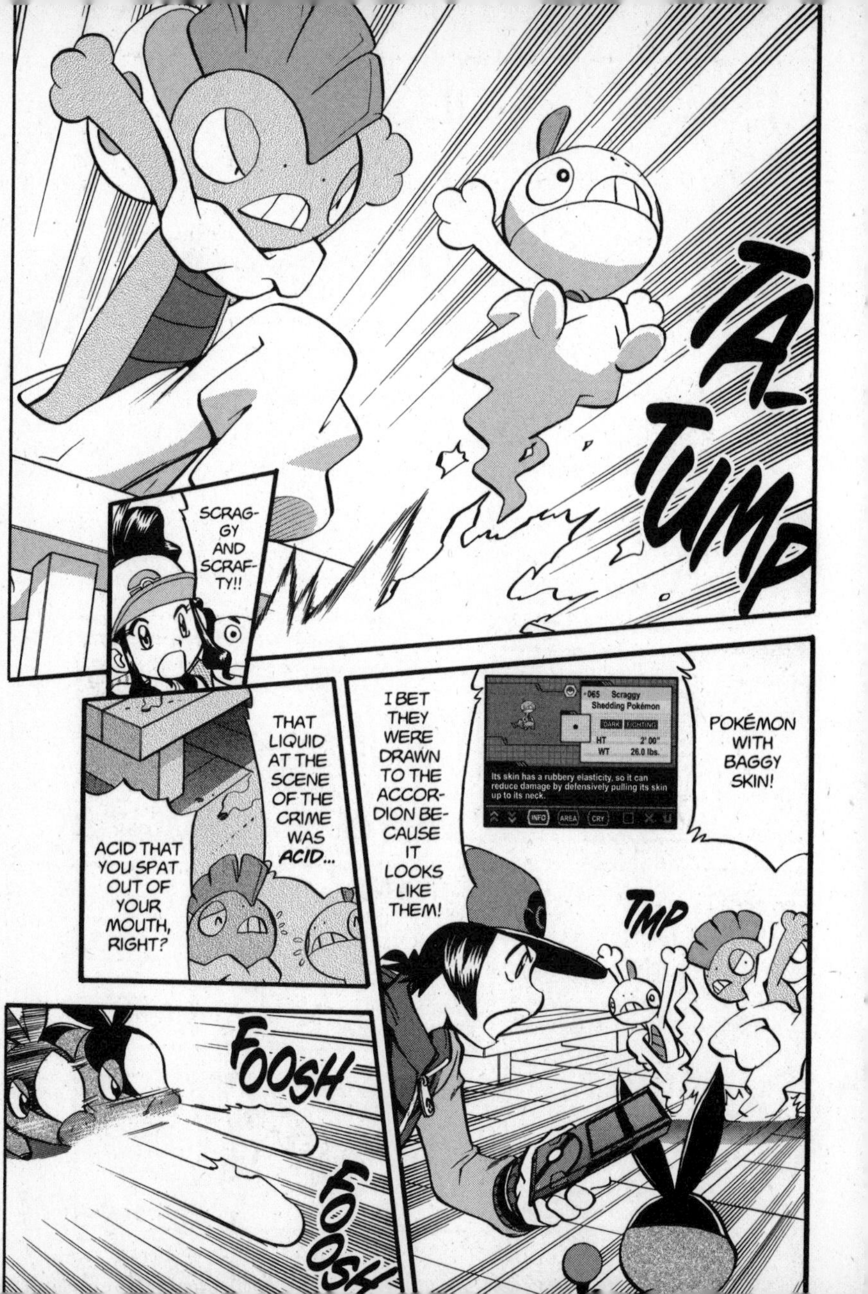
TA-TUMP
SCRAG-GY AND SCRAF-TY!!
POKÉMON WITH BAGGY SKIN!
065 Scraggy
Shedding Pokémon
DARK FIGHTING
HT 2' 00"
WT 26.0 lbs.
Its skin has a rubbery elasticity, so it can reduce damage by defensively pulling its skin up to its neck.
INFO AREA CRY
I BET THEY WERE DRAWN TO THE ACCOR-DION BE-CAUSE IT LOOKS LIKE THEM!
TMP
THAT LIQUID AT THE SCENE OF THE CRIME WAS *ACID*...
ACID THAT YOU SPAT OUT OF YOUR MOUTH, RIGHT?
FOOSH
FOOSH

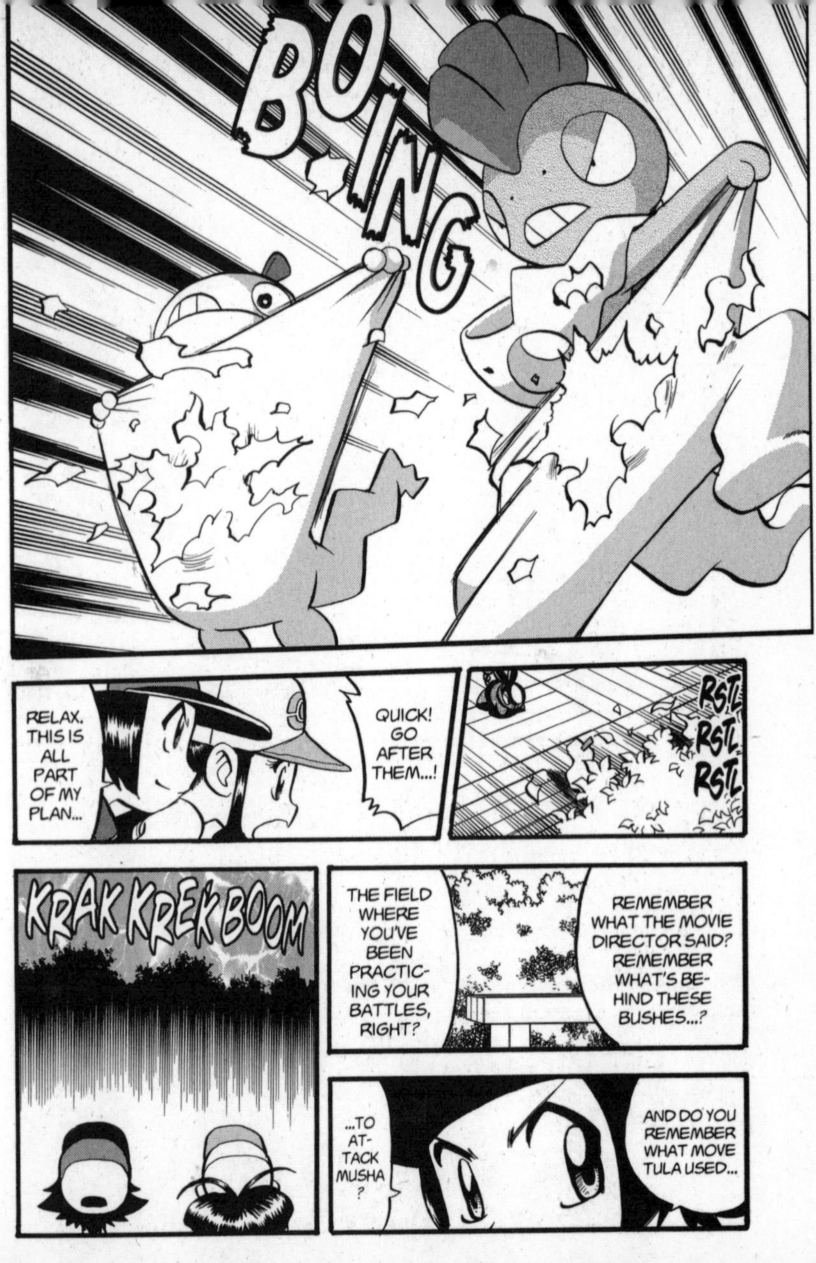
BOING
QUICK! GO AFTER THEM...!
RELAX. THIS IS ALL PART OF MY PLAN...
RSTL RSTL RSTL
KRAK KREK BOOM
REMEMBER WHAT THE MOVIE DIRECTOR SAID? REMEMBER WHAT'S BE-HIND THESE BUSHES...?
THE FIELD WHERE YOU'VE BEEN PRACTIC-ING YOUR BATTLES, RIGHT?
AND DO YOU REMEMBER WHAT MOVE TULA USED...
...TO AT-TACK MUSHA?

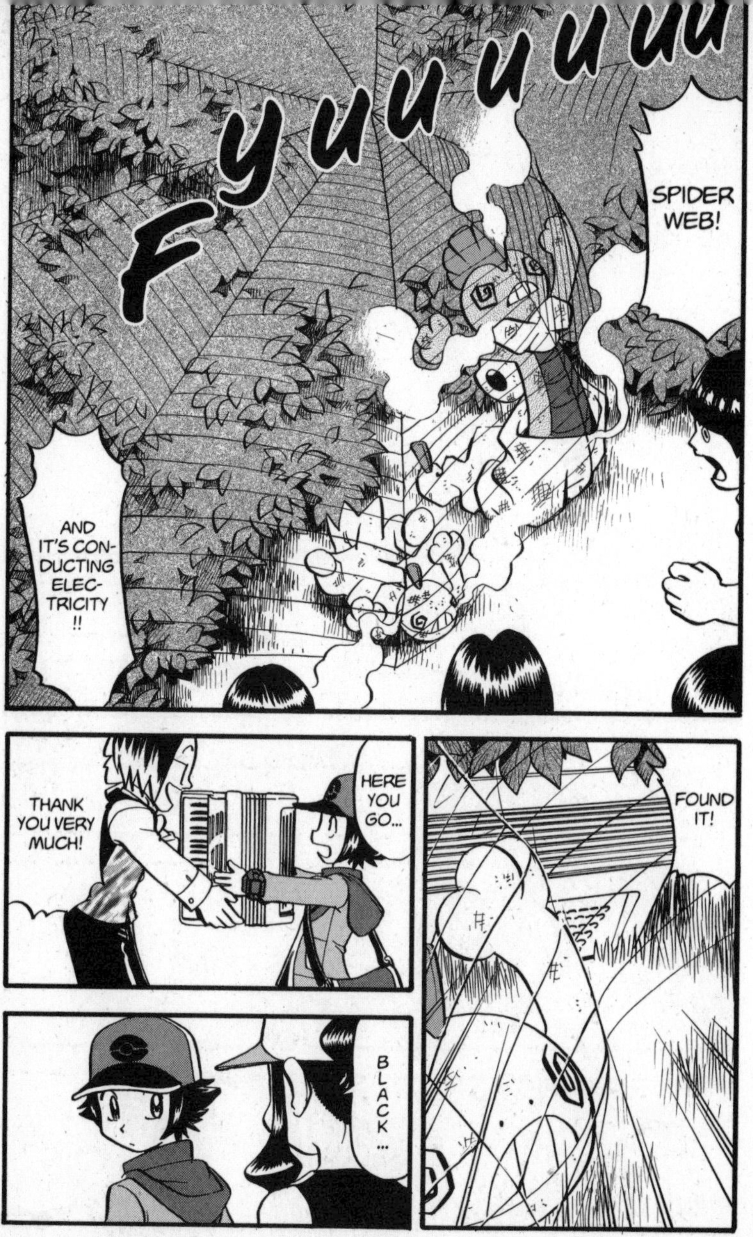
Fyuuuuuuu
SPIDER WEB!
AND IT'S CONDUCTING ELECTRICITY!!
FOUND IT!
HERE YOU GO...
THANK YOU VERY MUCH!
BLACK...

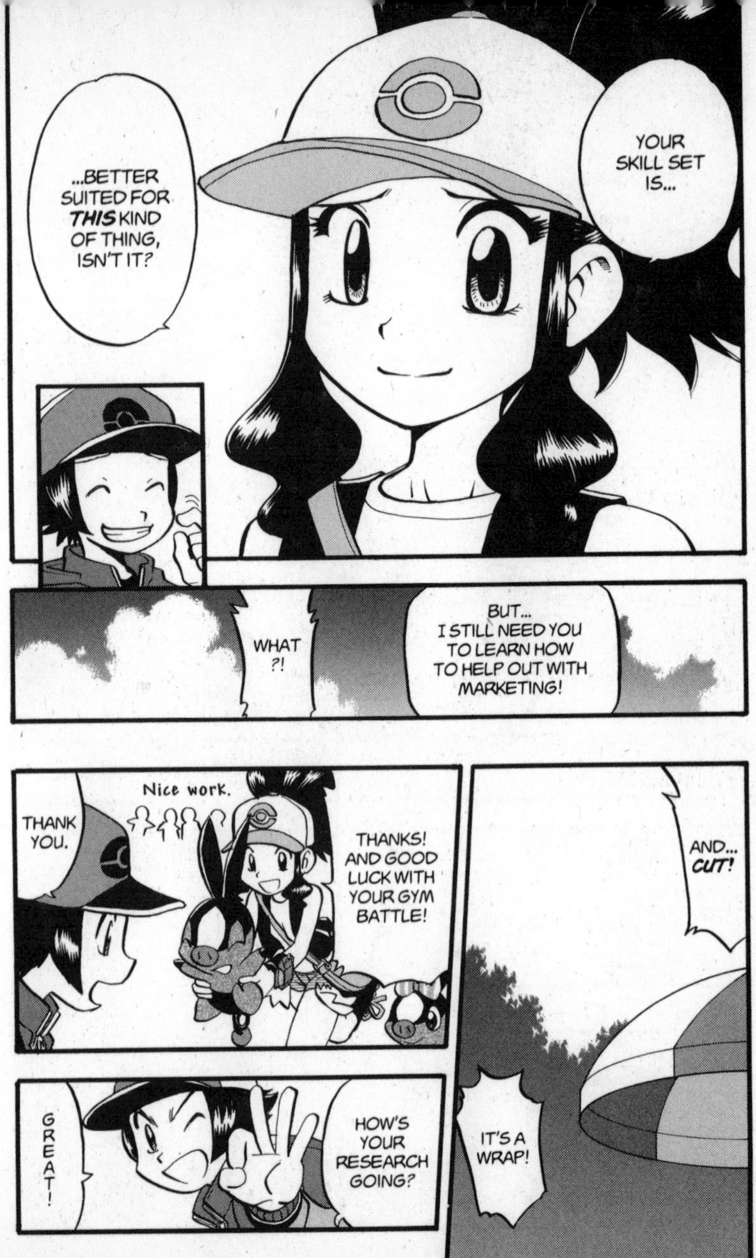
YOUR SKILL SET IS...
...BETTER SUITED FOR THIS KIND OF THING, ISN'T IT?
BUT... I STILL NEED YOU TO LEARN HOW TO HELP OUT WITH MARKETING!
WHAT ?!
AND... CUT!
THANKS! AND GOOD LUCK WITH YOUR GYM BATTLE!
Nice work.
THANK YOU.
IT'S A WRAP!
HOW'S YOUR RESEARCH GOING?
GREAT!

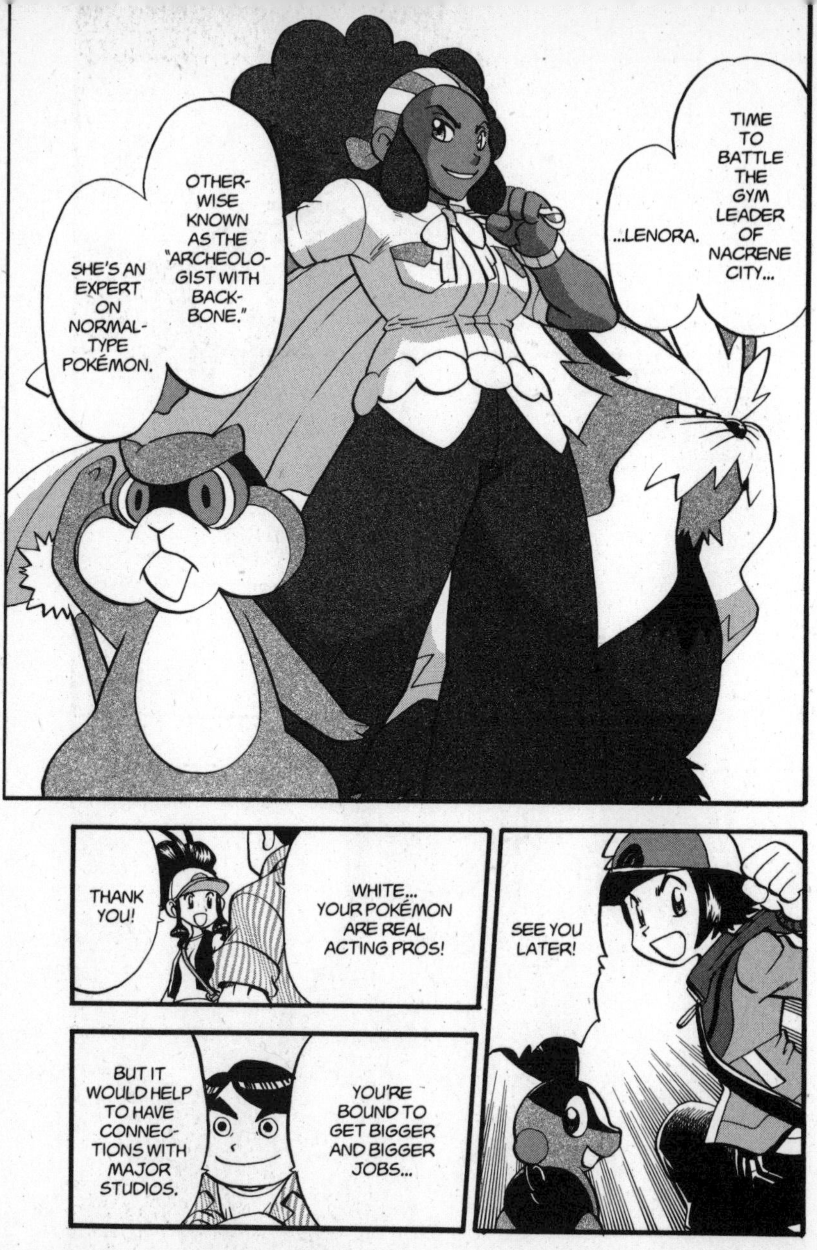
TIME TO BATTLE THE GYM LEADER OF NACRENE CITY...
...LENORA.
OTHER-WISE KNOWN AS THE "ARCHEOLO-GIST WITH BACK-BONE."
SHE'S AN EXPERT ON NORMAL-TYPE POKÉMON.
WHITE... YOUR POKÉMON ARE REAL ACTING PROS!
THANK YOU!
YOU'RE BOUND TO GET BIGGER AND BIGGER JOBS...
BUT IT WOULD HELP TO HAVE CONNECTIONS WITH MAJOR STUDIOS.
SEE YOU LATER!

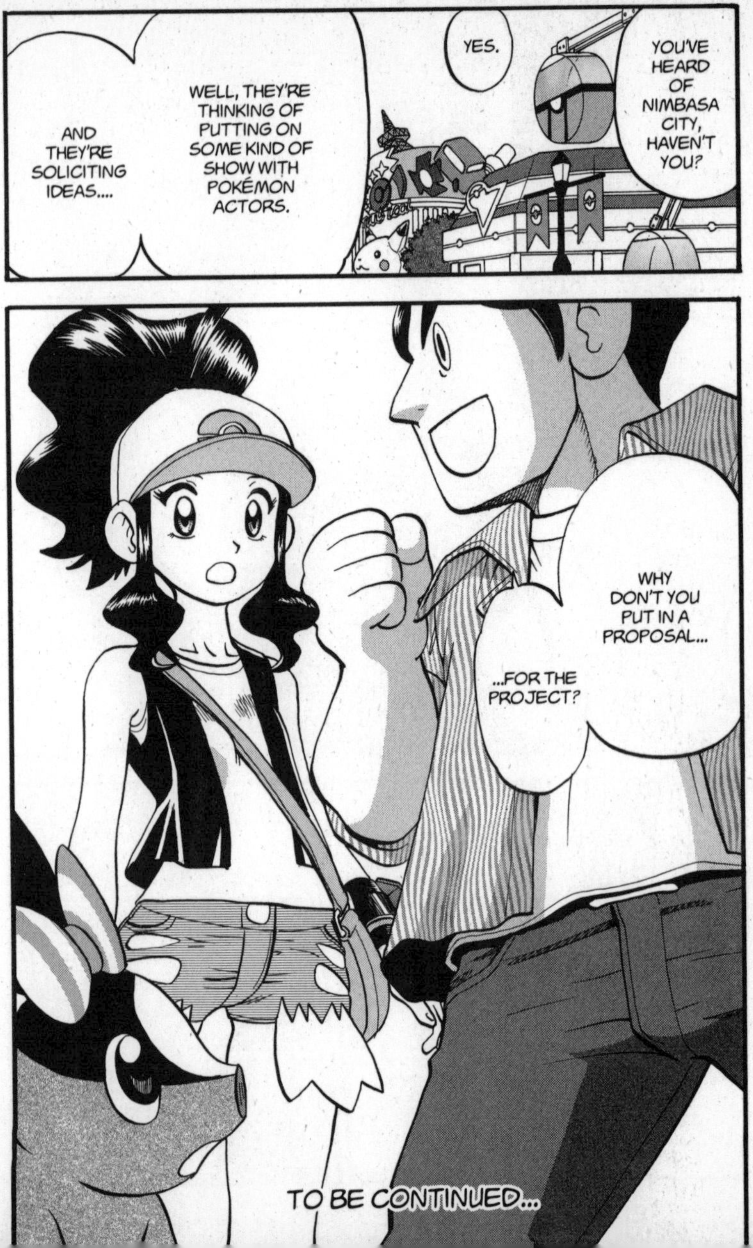
YOU'VE HEARD OF NIMBASA CITY, HAVEN'T YOU?
YES.
WELL, THEY'RE THINKING OF PUTTING ON SOME KIND OF SHOW WITH POKÉMON ACTORS.
AND THEY'RE SOLICITING IDEAS....
WHY DON'T YOU PUT IN A PROPOSAL...
...FOR THE PROJECT?
TO BE CONTINUED...

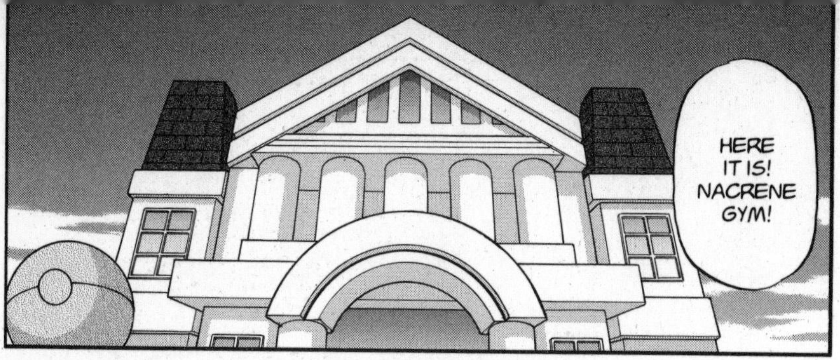
HERE IT IS! NACRENE GYM!

Adventure ⑬ Battle at the Museum

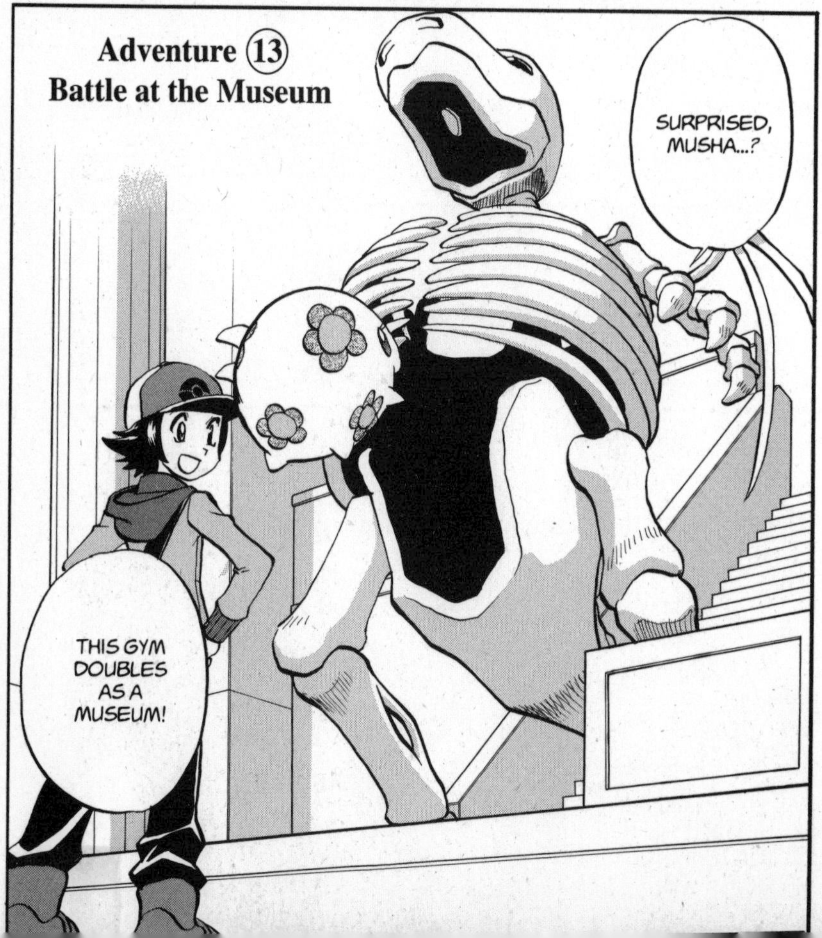
SURPRISED, MUSHA...?
THIS GYM DOUBLES AS A MUSEUM!

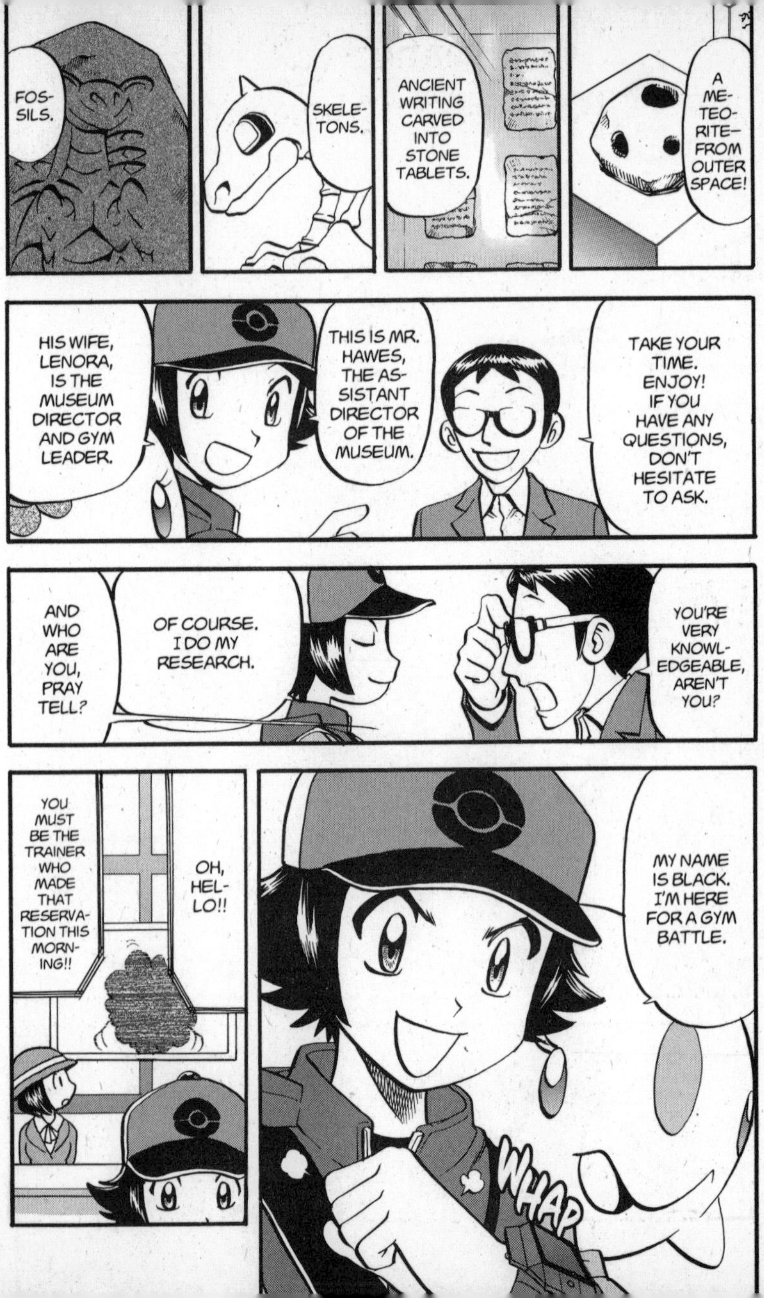
A METEORITE—FROM OUTER SPACE!
ANCIENT WRITING CARVED INTO STONE TABLETS.
SKELETONS.
FOSSILS.
TAKE YOUR TIME. ENJOY! IF YOU HAVE ANY QUESTIONS, DON'T HESITATE TO ASK.
THIS IS MR. HAWES, THE ASSISTANT DIRECTOR OF THE MUSEUM.
HIS WIFE, LENORA, IS THE MUSEUM DIRECTOR AND GYM LEADER.
YOU'RE VERY KNOWLEDGEABLE, AREN'T YOU?
OF COURSE. I DO MY RESEARCH.
AND WHO ARE YOU, PRAY TELL?
MY NAME IS BLACK. I'M HERE FOR A GYM BATTLE.
WHAP
OH, HELLO!!
YOU MUST BE THE TRAINER WHO MADE THAT RESERVATION THIS MORNING!!

Adventure 13
Battle at the Museum

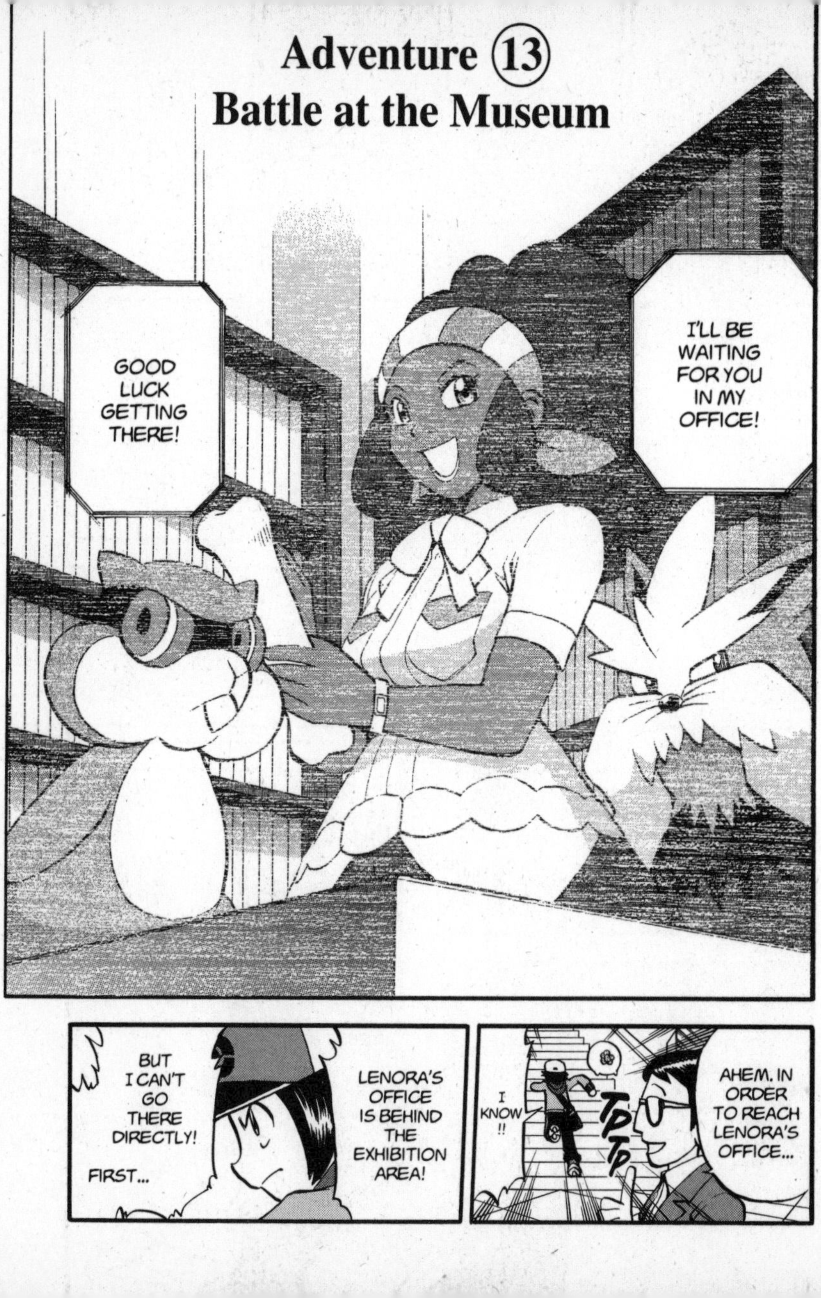
I'LL BE WAITING FOR YOU IN MY OFFICE!
GOOD LUCK GETTING THERE!
LENORA'S OFFICE IS BEHIND THE EXHIBITION AREA!
BUT I CAN'T GO THERE DIRECTLY!
FIRST...
AHEM. IN ORDER TO REACH LENORA'S OFFICE...
I KNOW !!
TPTP

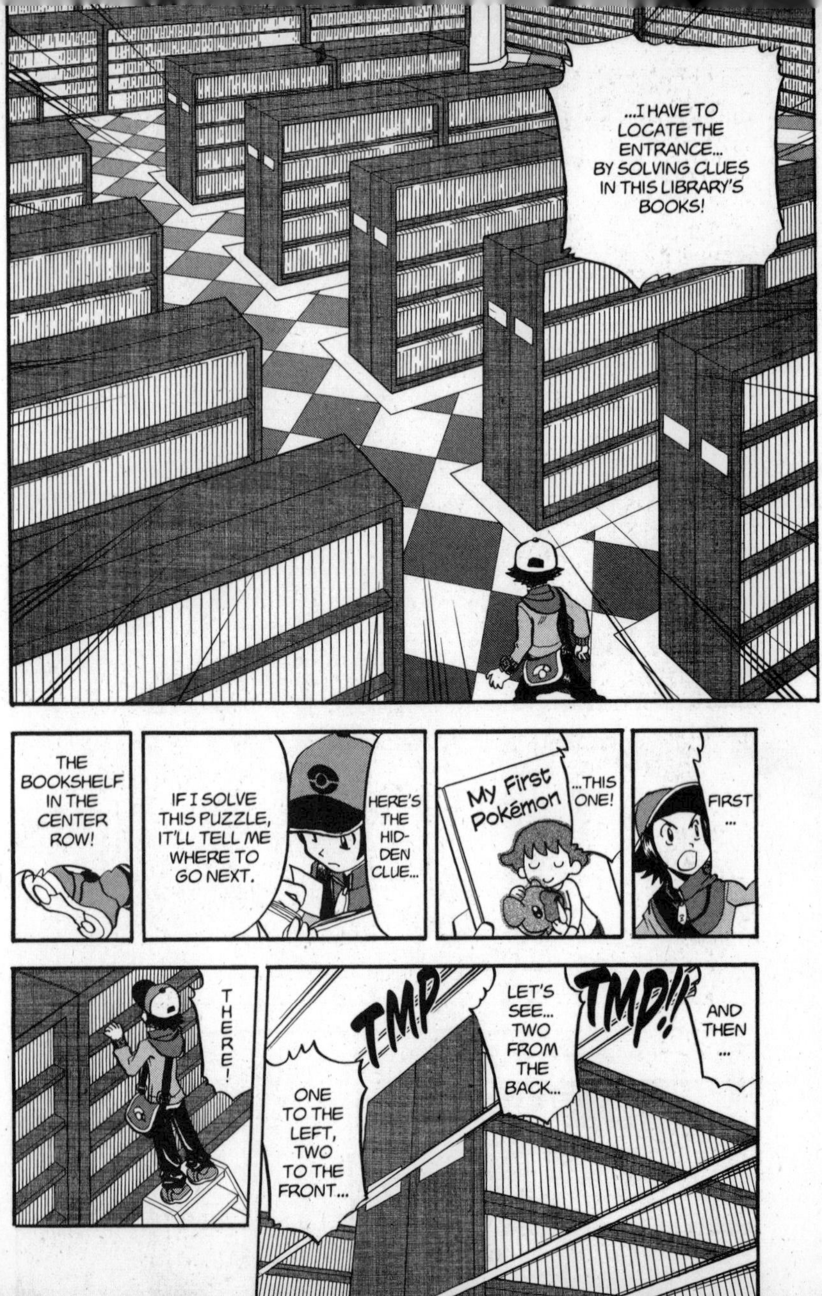
...I HAVE TO LOCATE THE ENTRANCE... BY SOLVING CLUES IN THIS LIBRARY'S BOOKS!
THE BOOKSHELF IN THE CENTER ROW!
IF I SOLVE THIS PUZZLE, IT'LL TELL ME WHERE TO GO NEXT.
HERE'S THE HID-DEN CLUE...
My First Pokémon
...THIS ONE!
FIRST...
THERE!
TMP
LET'S SEE... TWO FROM THE BACK...
ONE TO THE LEFT, TWO TO THE FRONT...
TMP!!
AND THEN...

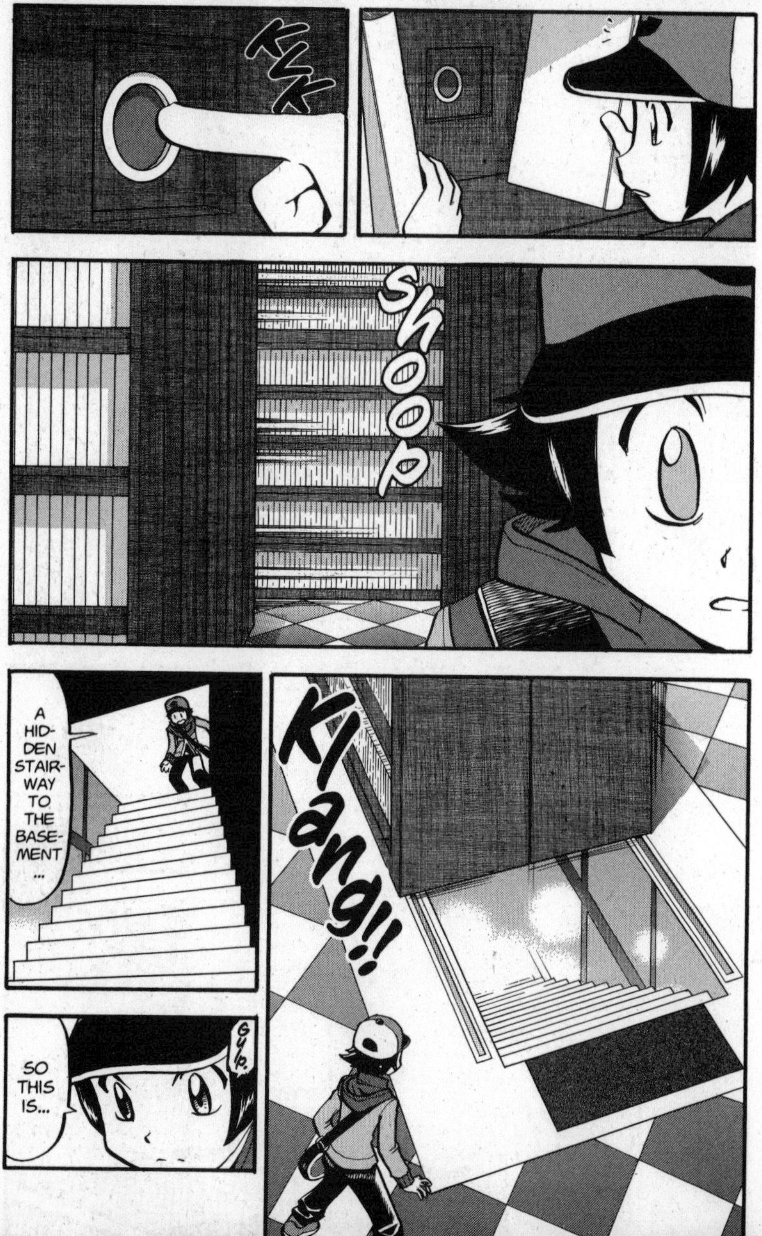
KLIK
SHOOOP
A HIDDEN STAIRWAY TO THE BASEMENT...
KLANG!!
GULP.
SO THIS IS...

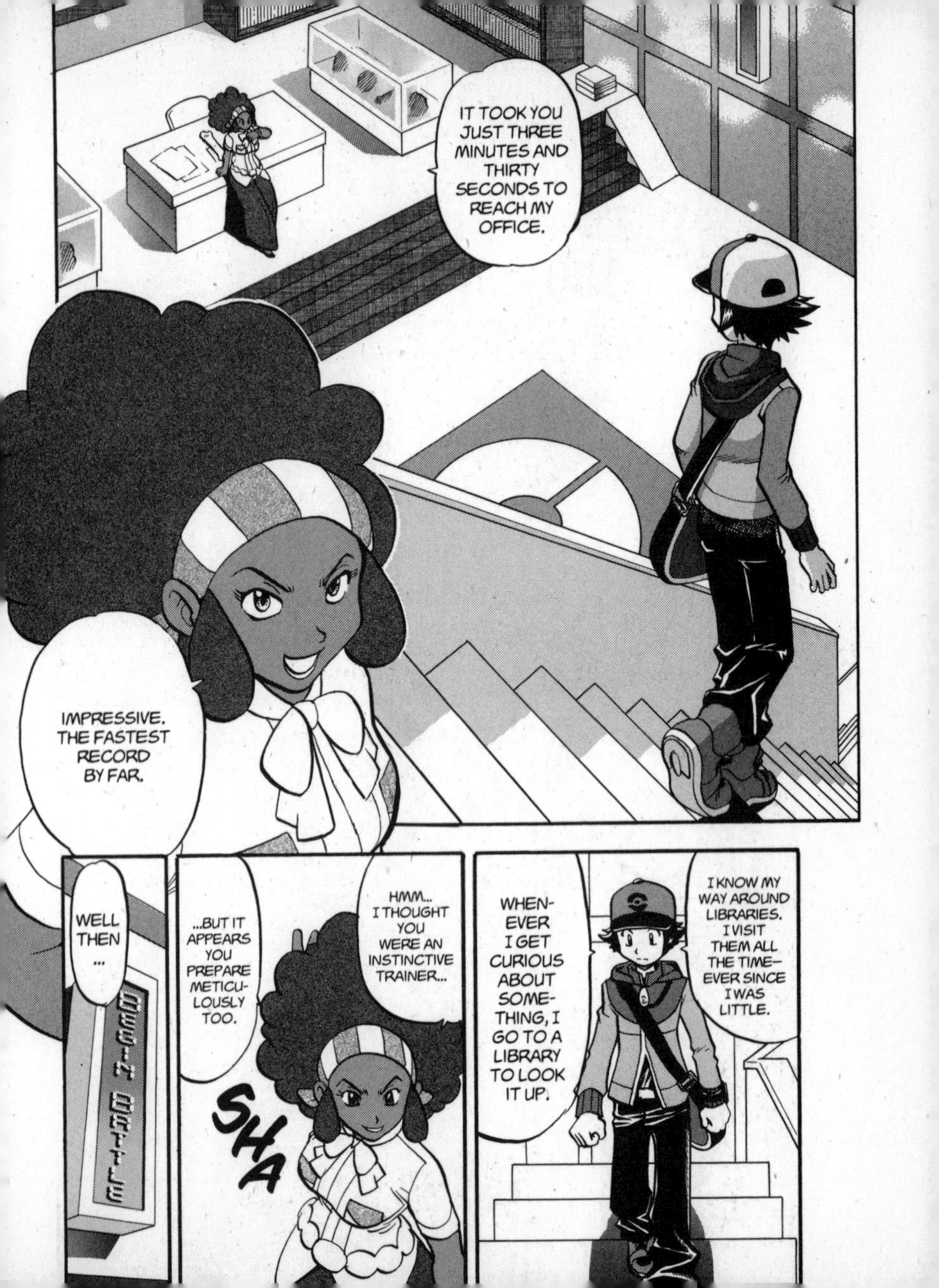
IT TOOK YOU JUST THREE MINUTES AND THIRTY SECONDS TO REACH MY OFFICE.
IMPRESSIVE. THE FASTEST RECORD BY FAR.
I KNOW MY WAY AROUND LIBRARIES. I VISIT THEM ALL THE TIME—EVER SINCE I WAS LITTLE.
WHEN-EVER I GET CURIOUS ABOUT SOME-THING, I GO TO A LIBRARY TO LOOK IT UP.
HMM... I THOUGHT YOU WERE AN INSTINCTIVE TRAINER...
...BUT IT APPEARS YOU PREPARE METICU-LOUSLY TOO.
SHA
WELL THEN ...
BEGIN BATTLE

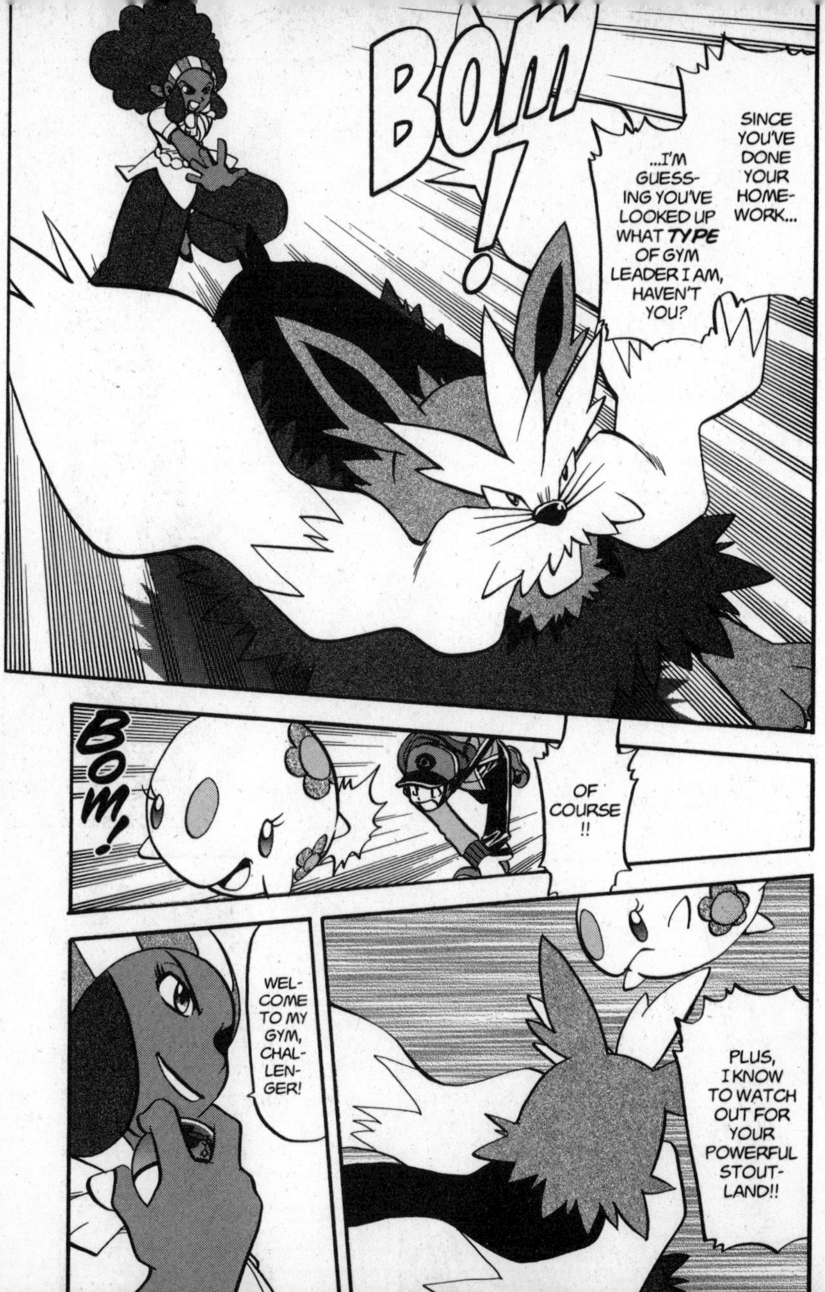
BOM!
SINCE YOU'VE DONE YOUR HOME-WORK...
...I'M GUESS-ING YOU'VE LOOKED UP WHAT TYPE OF GYM LEADER I AM, HAVEN'T YOU?
BOM!
OF COURSE !!
PLUS, I KNOW TO WATCH OUT FOR YOUR POWERFUL STOUT-LAND!!
WEL-COME TO MY GYM, CHAL-LEN-GER!

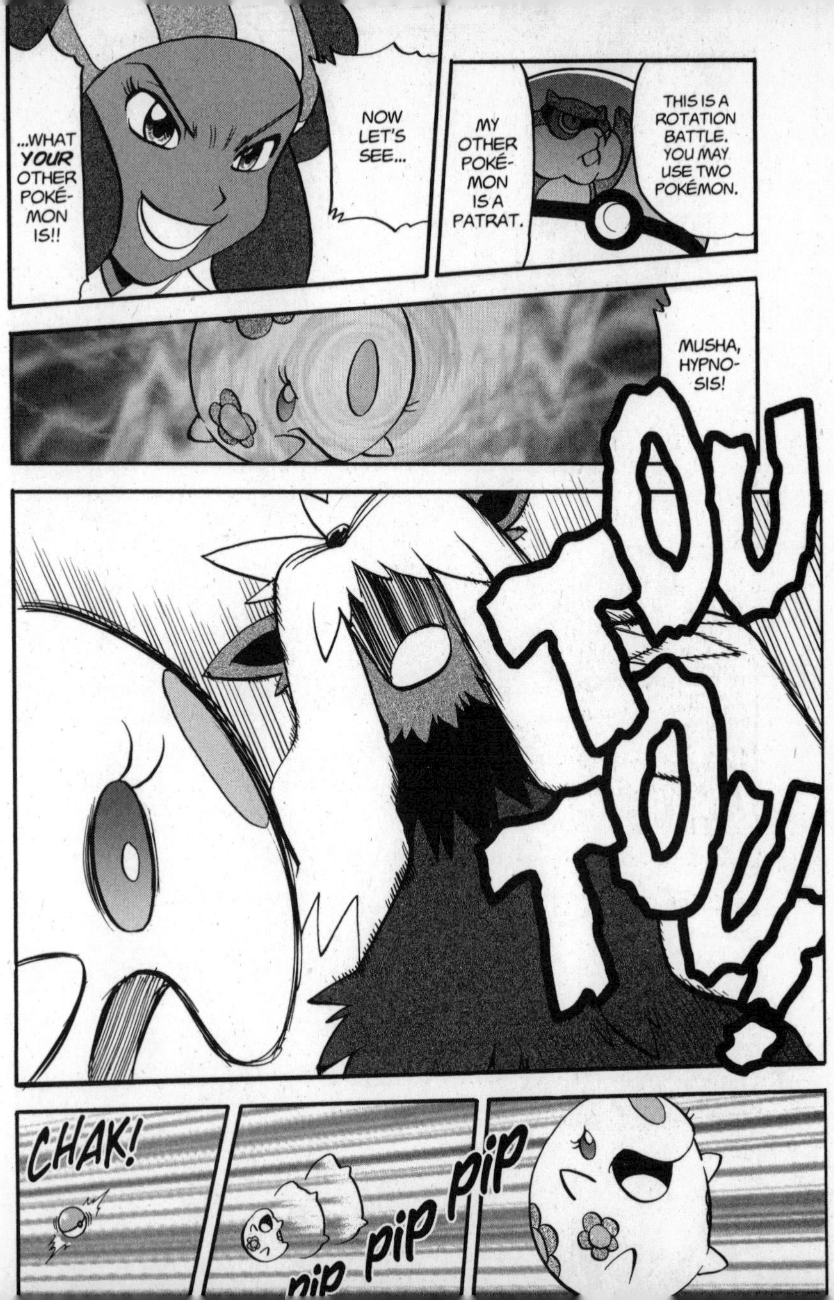
THIS IS A ROTATION BATTLE. YOU MAY USE TWO POKÉMON.
MY OTHER POKÉMON IS A PATRAT.
NOW LET'S SEE...
...WHAT YOUR OTHER POKÉMON IS!!
MUSHA, HYPNOSIS!
TOU TOU TOU
pip pip pip
CHAK!

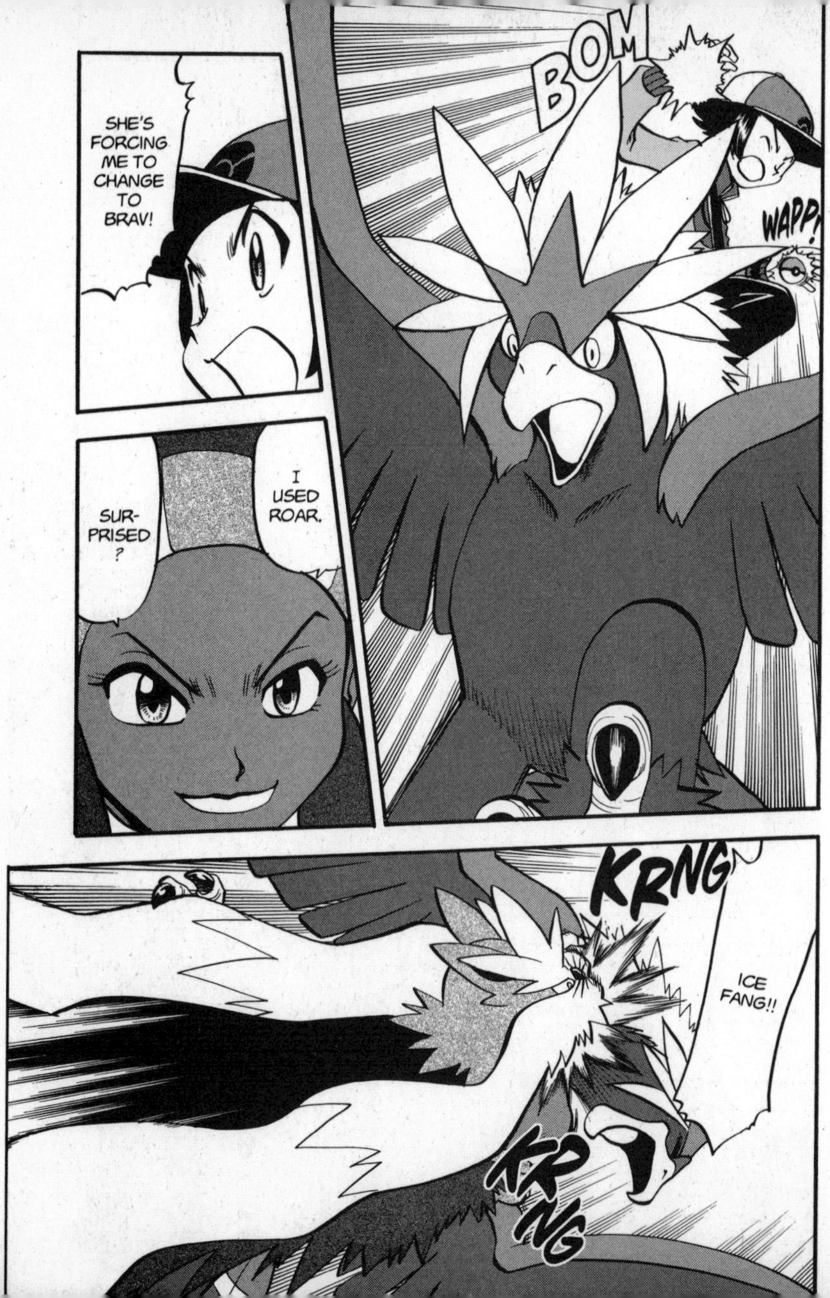
SHE'S FORCING ME TO CHANGE TO BRAV!
BOM
WAPP!
I USED ROAR.
SUR-PRISED?
KRNG
ICE FANG!!
KRNG

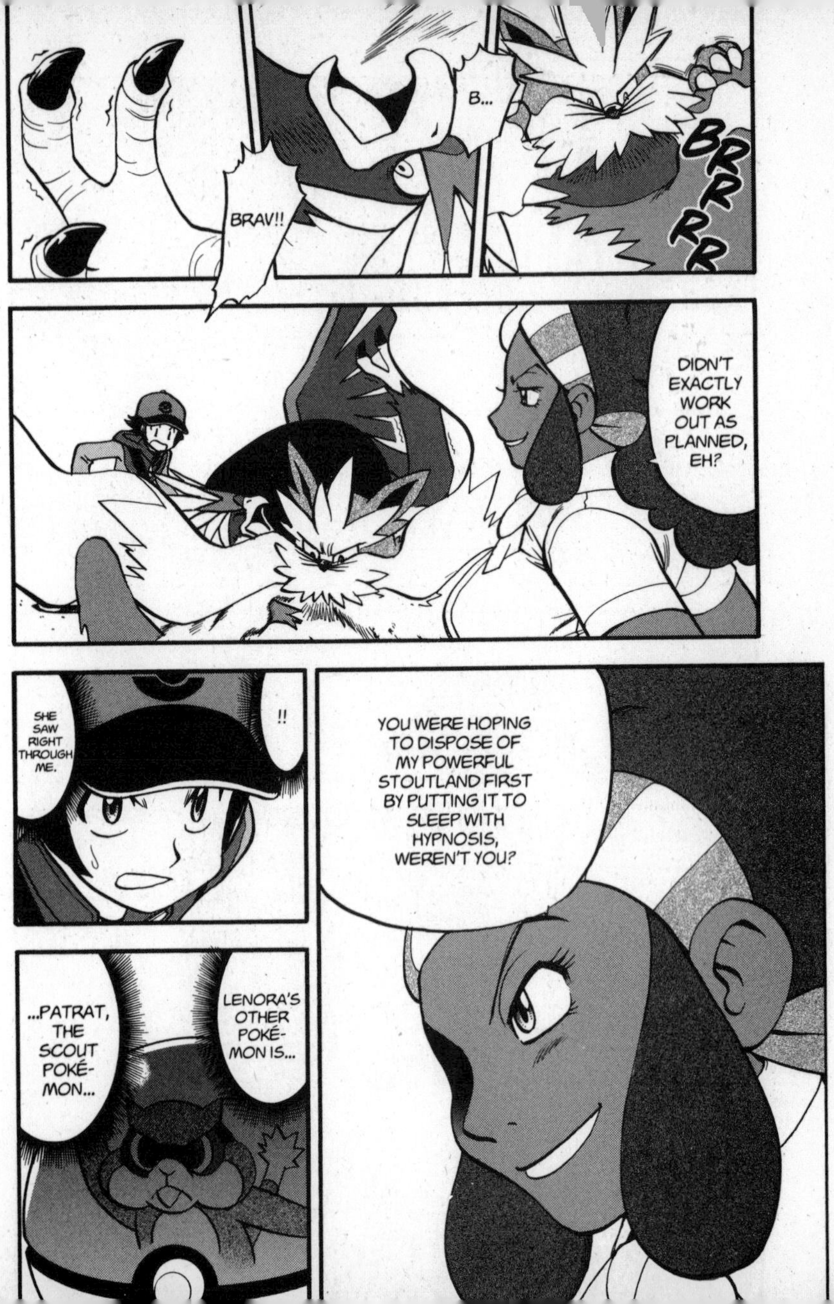
B...
BRRRRR
BRAV!!
DIDN'T EXACTLY WORK OUT AS PLANNED, EH?
!!
SHE SAW RIGHT THROUGH ME.
YOU WERE HOPING TO DISPOSE OF MY POWERFUL STOUTLAND FIRST BY PUTTING IT TO SLEEP WITH HYPNOSIS, WEREN'T YOU?
LENORA'S OTHER POKÉ-MON IS...
...PATRAT, THE SCOUT POKÉ-MON...

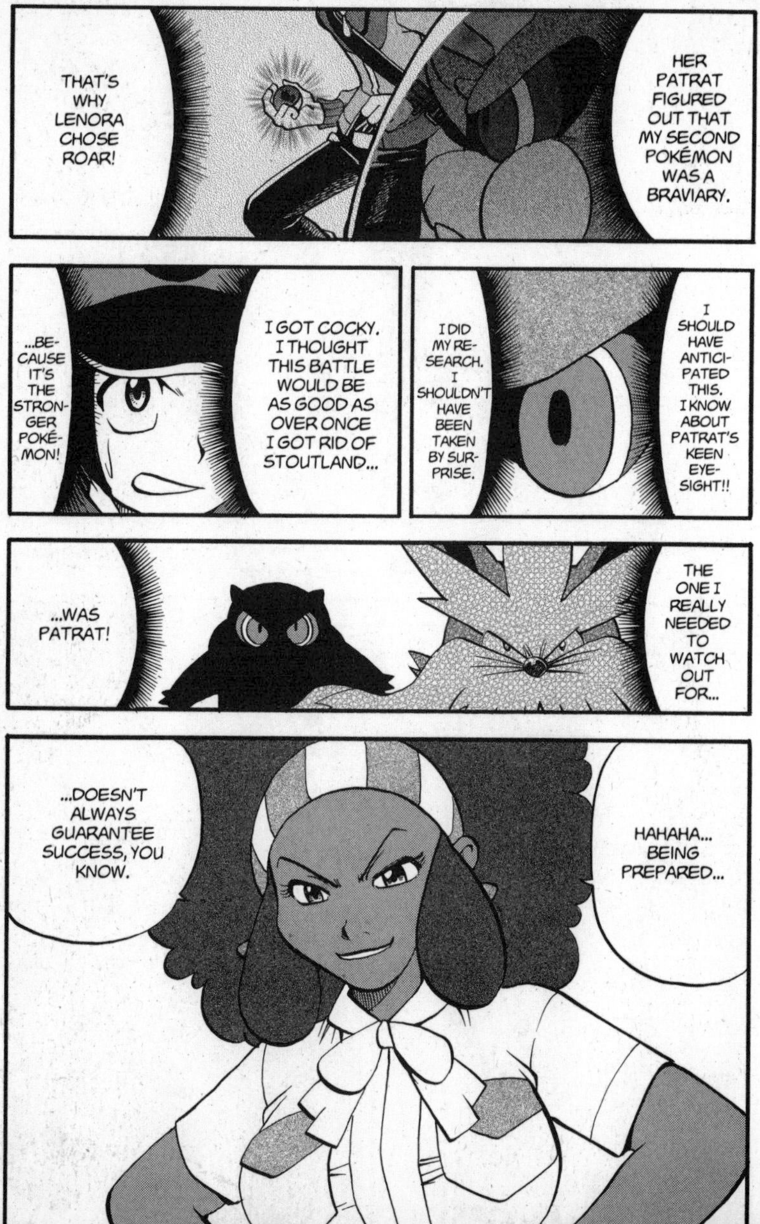
HER PATRAT FIGURED OUT THAT MY SECOND POKÉMON WAS A BRAVIARY.
THAT'S WHY LENORA CHOSE ROAR!
I SHOULD HAVE ANTICIPATED THIS. I KNOW ABOUT PATRAT'S KEEN EYESIGHT!!
I DID MY RESEARCH. I SHOULDN'T HAVE BEEN TAKEN BY SURPRISE.
I GOT COCKY. I THOUGHT THIS BATTLE WOULD BE AS GOOD AS OVER ONCE I GOT RID OF STOUTLAND...
...BECAUSE IT'S THE STRONGER POKÉMON!
THE ONE I REALLY NEEDED TO WATCH OUT FOR...
...WAS PATRAT!
HAHAHA... BEING PREPARED...
...DOESN'T ALWAYS GUARANTEE SUCCESS, YOU KNOW.

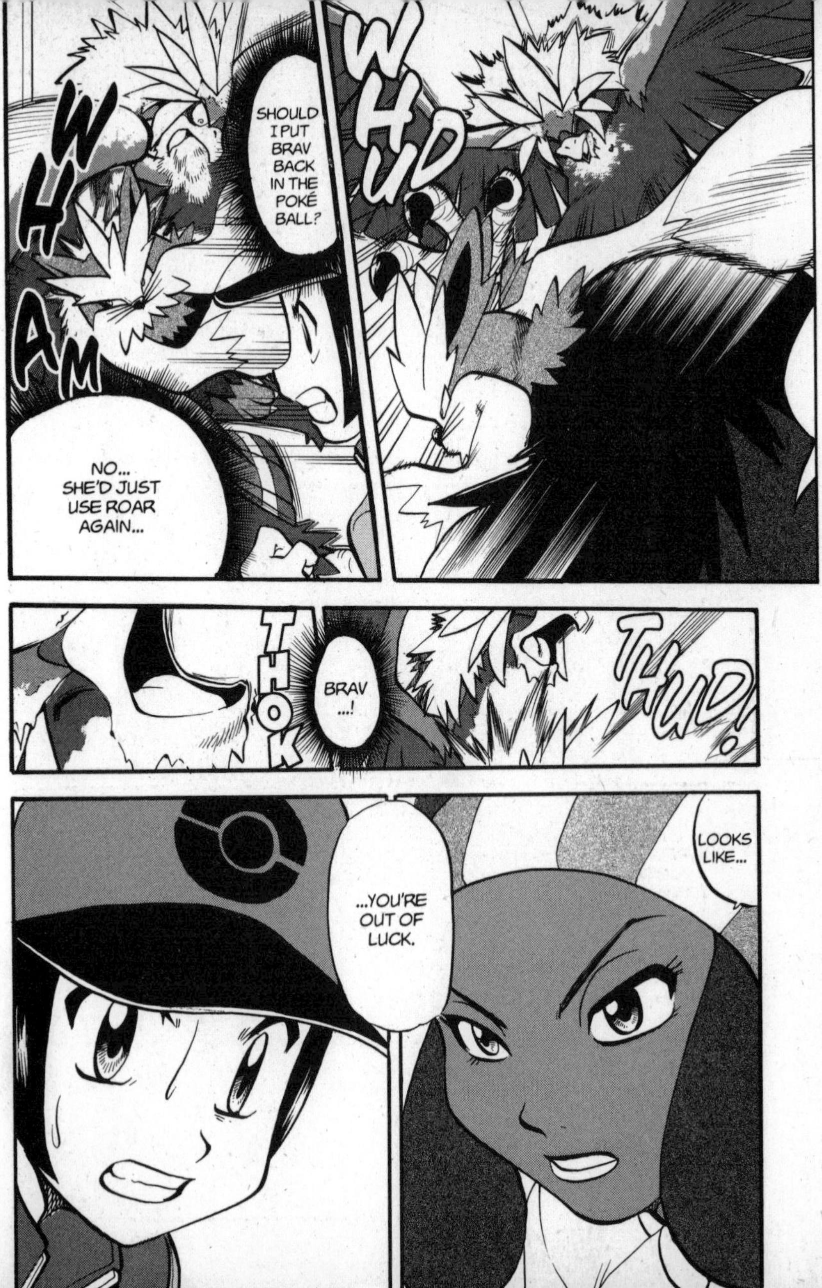
WHAM
WHUD
SHOULD I PUT BRAV BACK IN THE POKÉ BALL?
NO... SHE'D JUST USE ROAR AGAIN...
THUD!
BRAV...!
THOK
LOOKS LIKE...
...YOU'RE OUT OF LUCK.

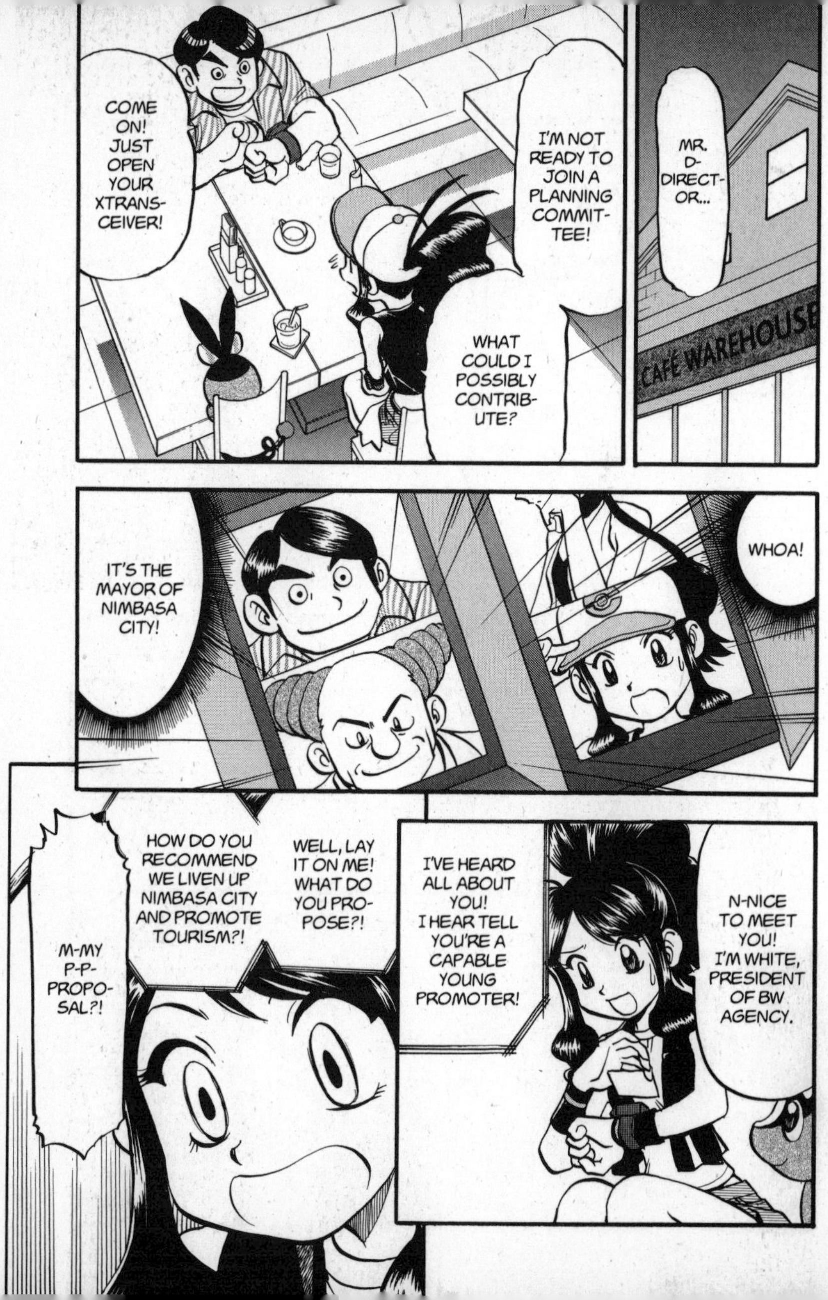
MR. D-DIRECTOR...
CAFÉ WAREHOUSE
I'M NOT READY TO JOIN A PLANNING COMMITTEE!
WHAT COULD I POSSIBLY CONTRIBUTE?
COME ON! JUST OPEN YOUR XTRANSCEIVER!
WHOA!
IT'S THE MAYOR OF NIMBASA CITY!
N-NICE TO MEET YOU! I'M WHITE, PRESIDENT OF BW AGENCY.
I'VE HEARD ALL ABOUT YOU! I HEAR TELL YOU'RE A CAPABLE YOUNG PROMOTER!
WELL, LAY IT ON ME! WHAT DO YOU PROPOSE?!
HOW DO YOU RECOMMEND WE LIVEN UP NIMBASA CITY AND PROMOTE TOURISM?!
M-MY P-P-PROPOSAL?!

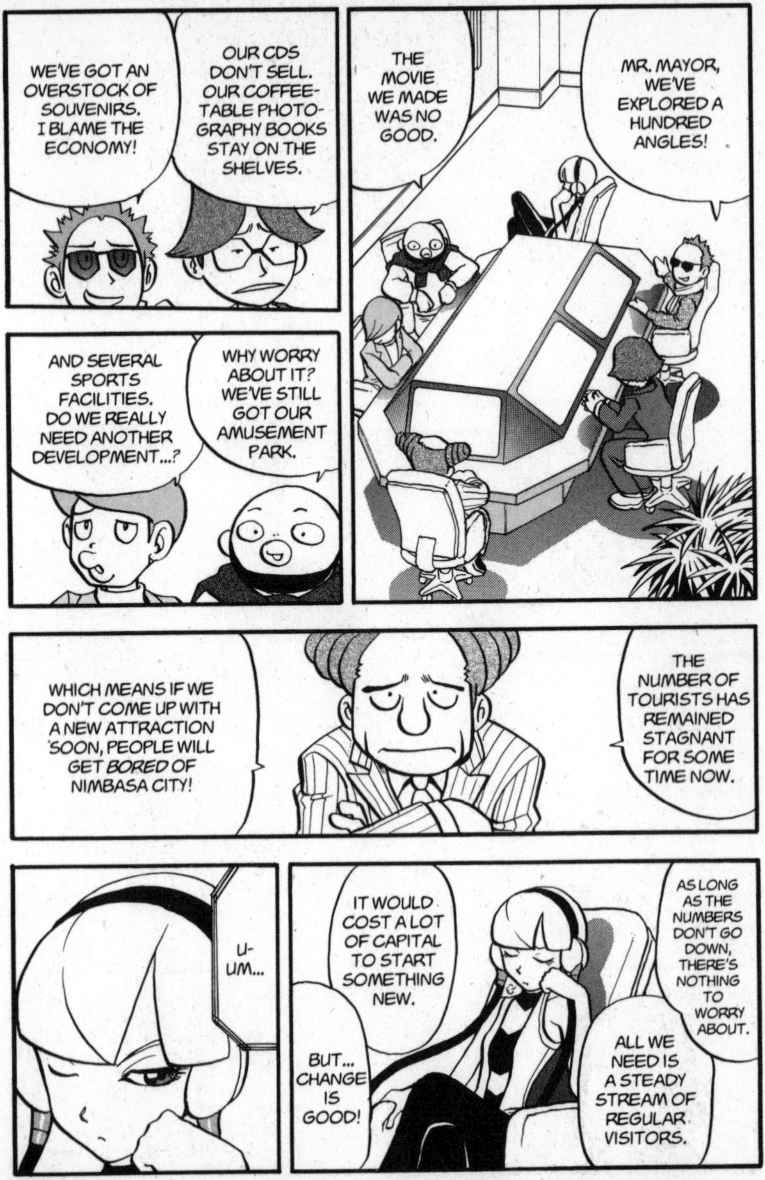
MR. MAYOR, WE'VE EXPLORED A HUNDRED ANGLES!
THE MOVIE WE MADE WAS NO GOOD.
OUR CDS DON'T SELL. OUR COFFEE-TABLE PHOTOGRAPHY BOOKS STAY ON THE SHELVES.
WE'VE GOT AN OVERSTOCK OF SOUVENIRS. I BLAME THE ECONOMY!
AND SEVERAL SPORTS FACILITIES. DO WE REALLY NEED ANOTHER DEVELOPMENT...?
WHY WORRY ABOUT IT? WE'VE STILL GOT OUR AMUSEMENT PARK.
THE NUMBER OF TOURISTS HAS REMAINED STAGNANT FOR SOME TIME NOW.
WHICH MEANS IF WE DON'T COME UP WITH A NEW ATTRACTION SOON, PEOPLE WILL GET *BORED* OF NIMBASA CITY!
AS LONG AS THE NUMBERS DON'T GO DOWN, THERE'S NOTHING TO WORRY ABOUT.
IT WOULD COST A LOT OF CAPITAL TO START SOMETHING NEW.
ALL WE NEED IS A STEADY STREAM OF REGULAR VISITORS.
BUT... CHANGE IS GOOD!
U-UM...

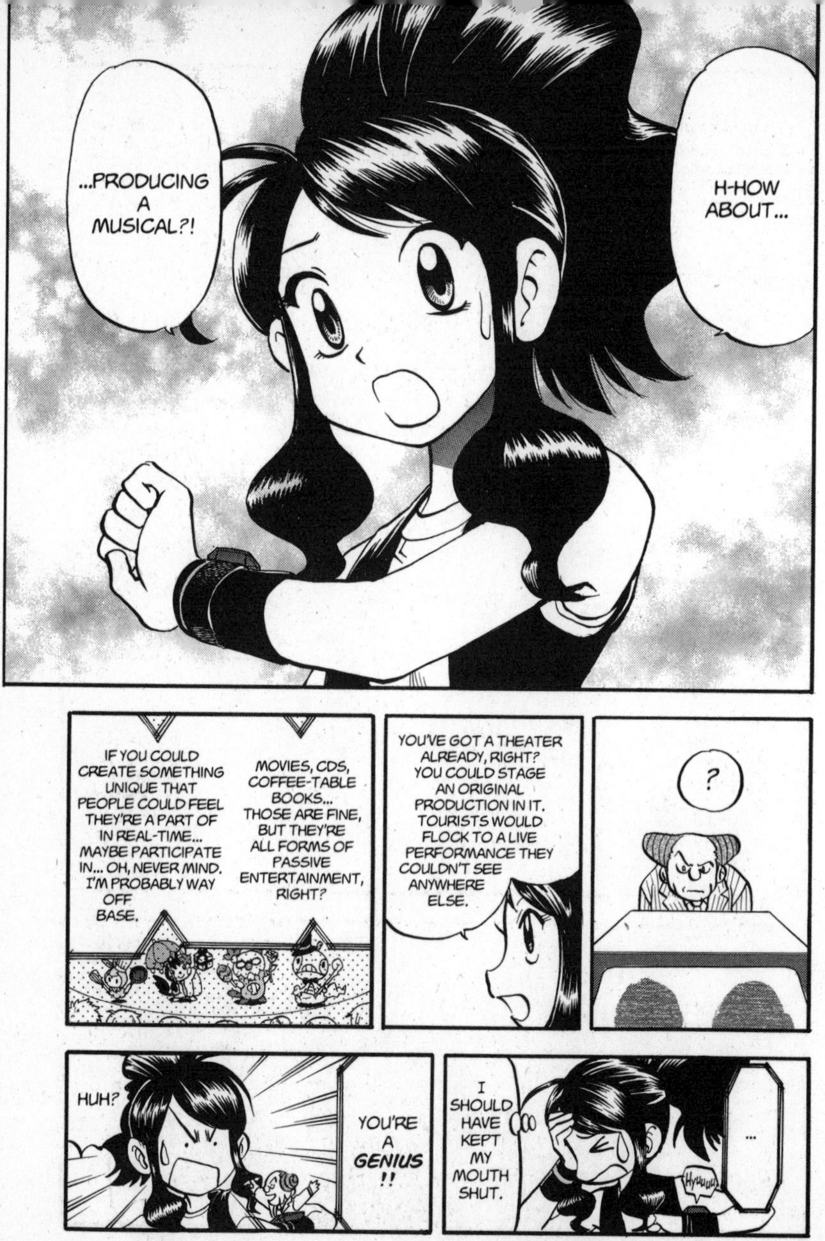
H-HOW ABOUT...
...PRODUCING A MUSICAL?!
?
YOU'VE GOT A THEATER ALREADY, RIGHT? YOU COULD STAGE AN ORIGINAL PRODUCTION IN IT. TOURISTS WOULD FLOCK TO A LIVE PERFORMANCE THEY COULDN'T SEE ANYWHERE ELSE.
MOVIES, CDS, COFFEE-TABLE BOOKS... THOSE ARE FINE, BUT THEY'RE ALL FORMS OF PASSIVE ENTERTAINMENT, RIGHT?
IF YOU COULD CREATE SOMETHING UNIQUE THAT PEOPLE COULD FEEL THEY'RE A PART OF IN REAL-TIME... MAYBE PARTICIPATE IN... OH, NEVER MIND. I'M PROBABLY WAY OFF BASE.
...
I SHOULD HAVE KEPT MY MOUTH SHUT.
YOU'RE A GENIUS!!
HUH?

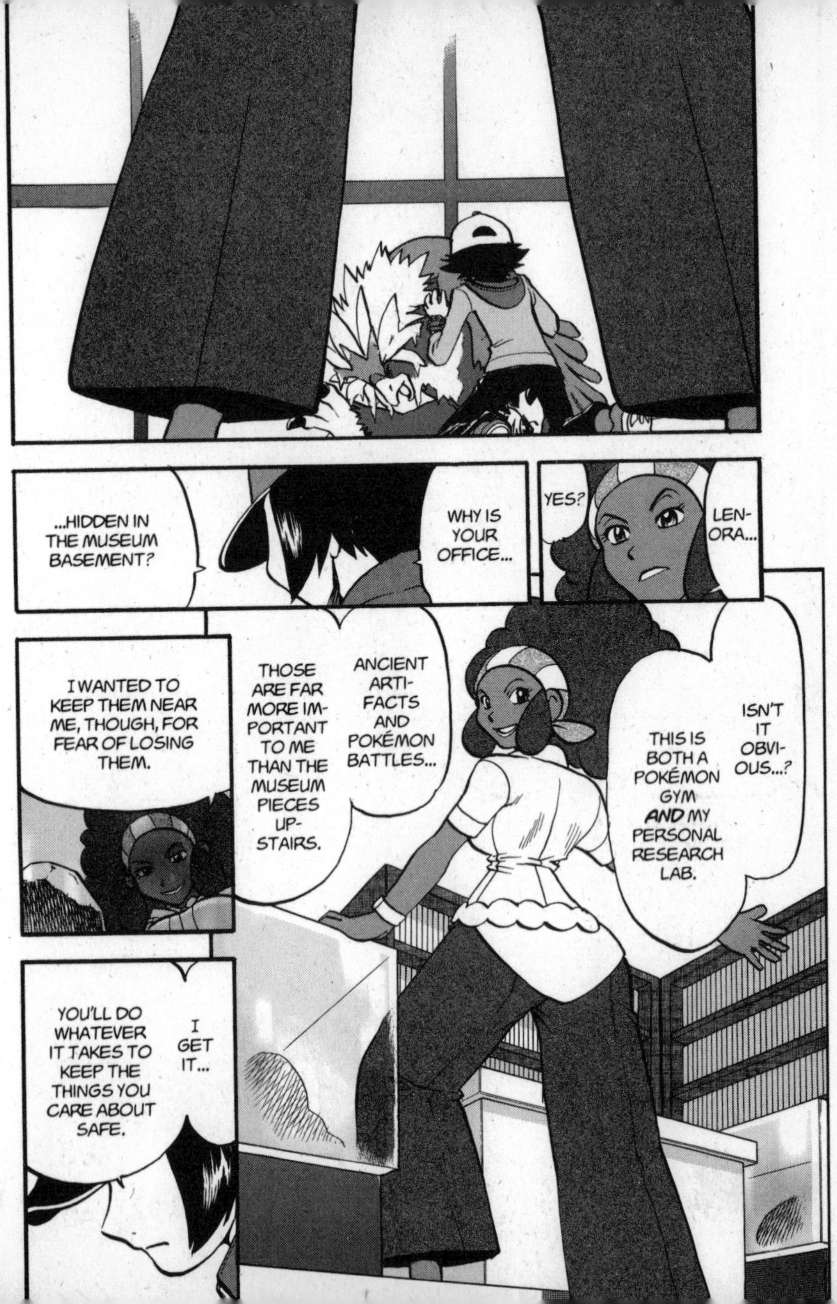
LEN-ORA...
YES?
WHY IS YOUR OFFICE...
...HIDDEN IN THE MUSEUM BASEMENT?
ISN'T IT OBVIOUS...?
THIS IS BOTH A POKÉMON GYM ***AND*** MY PERSONAL RESEARCH LAB.
ANCIENT ARTIFACTS AND POKÉMON BATTLES...
THOSE ARE FAR MORE IMPORTANT TO ME THAN THE MUSEUM PIECES UPSTAIRS.
I WANTED TO KEEP THEM NEAR ME, THOUGH, FOR FEAR OF LOSING THEM.
I GET IT...
YOU'LL DO WHATEVER IT TAKES TO KEEP THE THINGS YOU CARE ABOUT SAFE.

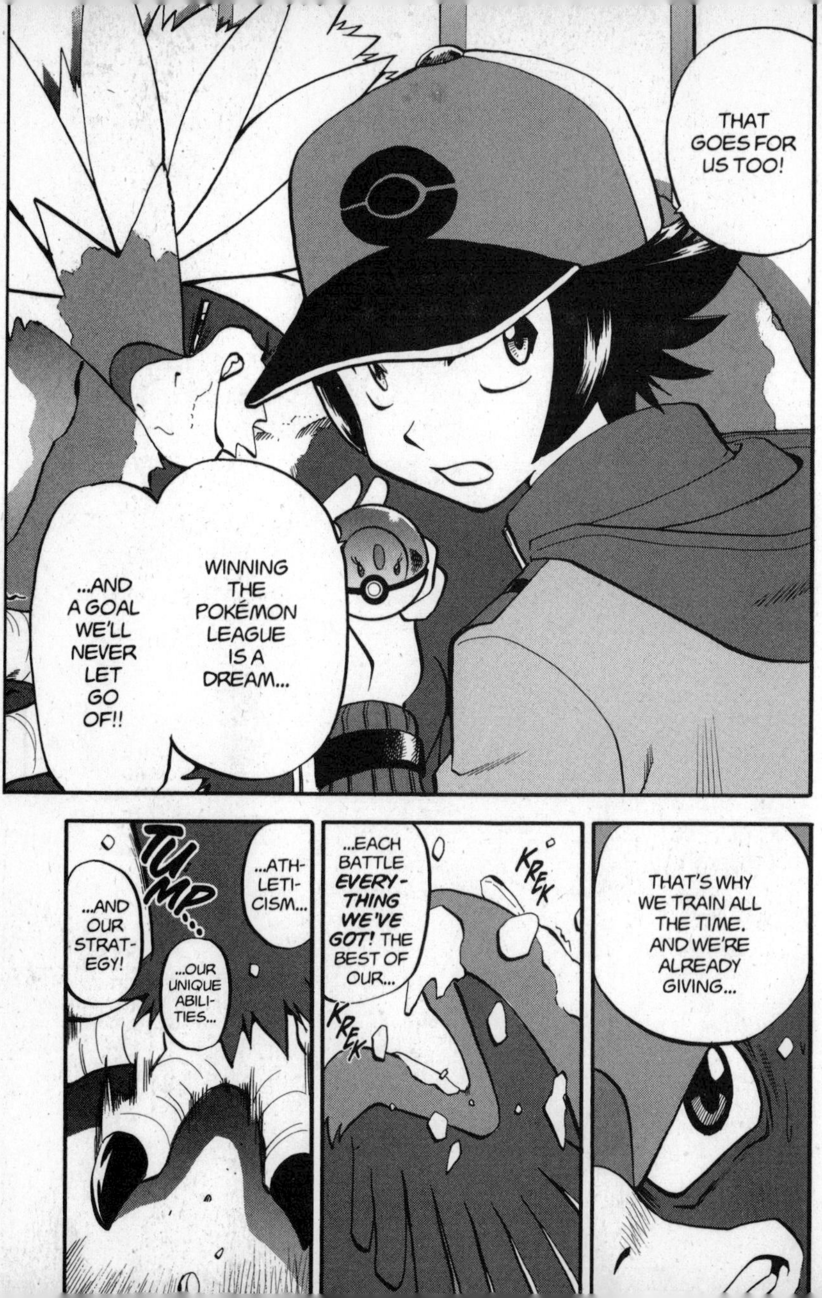
THAT GOES FOR US TOO!
WINNING THE POKÉMON LEAGUE IS A DREAM...
...AND A GOAL WE'LL NEVER LET GO OF!!
THAT'S WHY WE TRAIN ALL THE TIME. AND WE'RE ALREADY GIVING...
...EACH BATTLE ***EVERYTHING WE'VE GOT!*** THE BEST OF OUR...
KREK
KREK
...ATH-LETI-CISM...
...OUR UNIQUE ABILI-TIES...
...AND OUR STRAT-EGY!
TUMP...

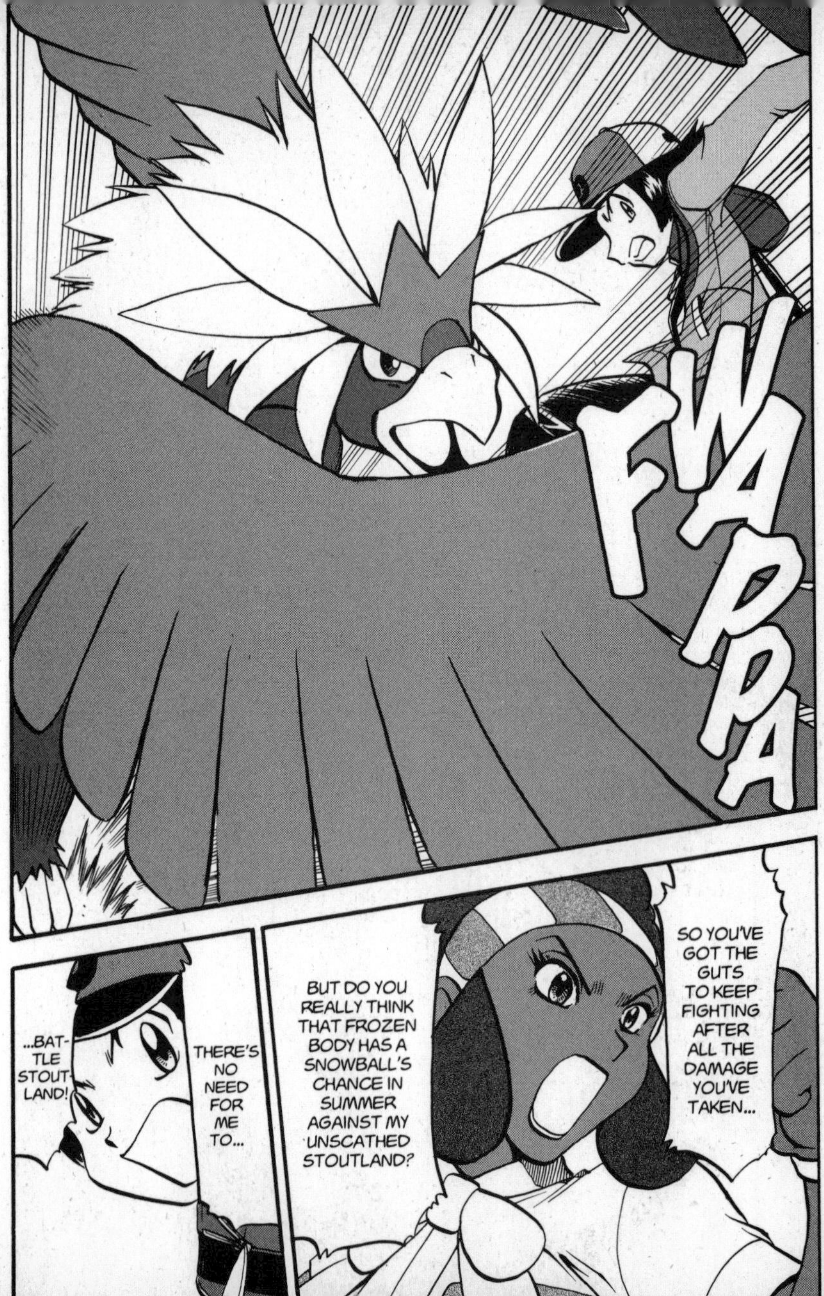

FWAPPA
SO YOU'VE GOT THE GUTS TO KEEP FIGHTING AFTER ALL THE DAMAGE YOU'VE TAKEN...
BUT DO YOU REALLY THINK THAT FROZEN BODY HAS A SNOWBALL'S CHANCE IN SUMMER AGAINST MY UNSCATHED STOUTLAND?
THERE'S NO NEED FOR ME TO...
...BAT-TLE STOUT-LAND!

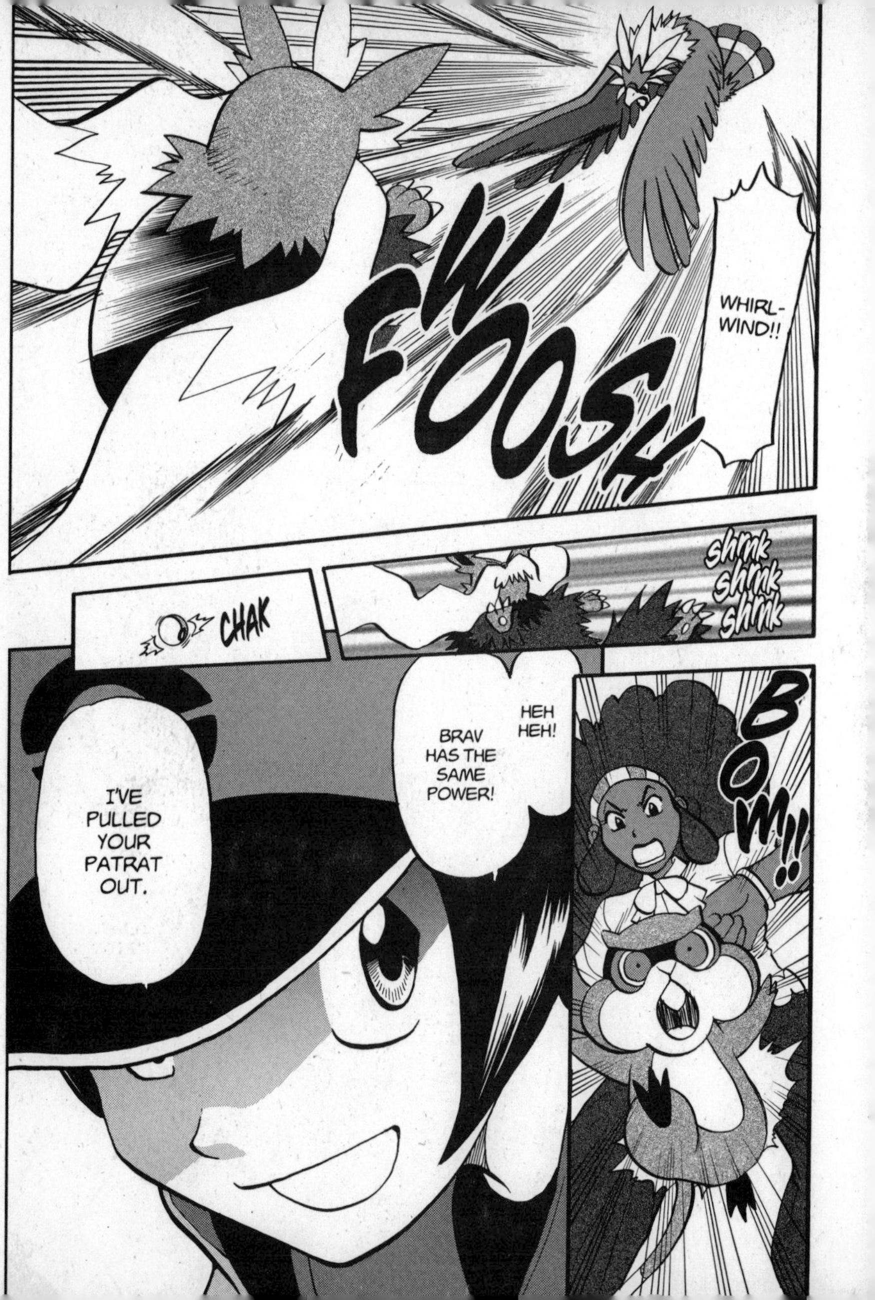
WHIRL-WIND!!
FWOOSH
CHAK
shrnk shrnk shrnk
BRAV HAS THE SAME POWER!
HEH HEH!
I'VE PULLED YOUR PATRAT OUT.
BOOM!!

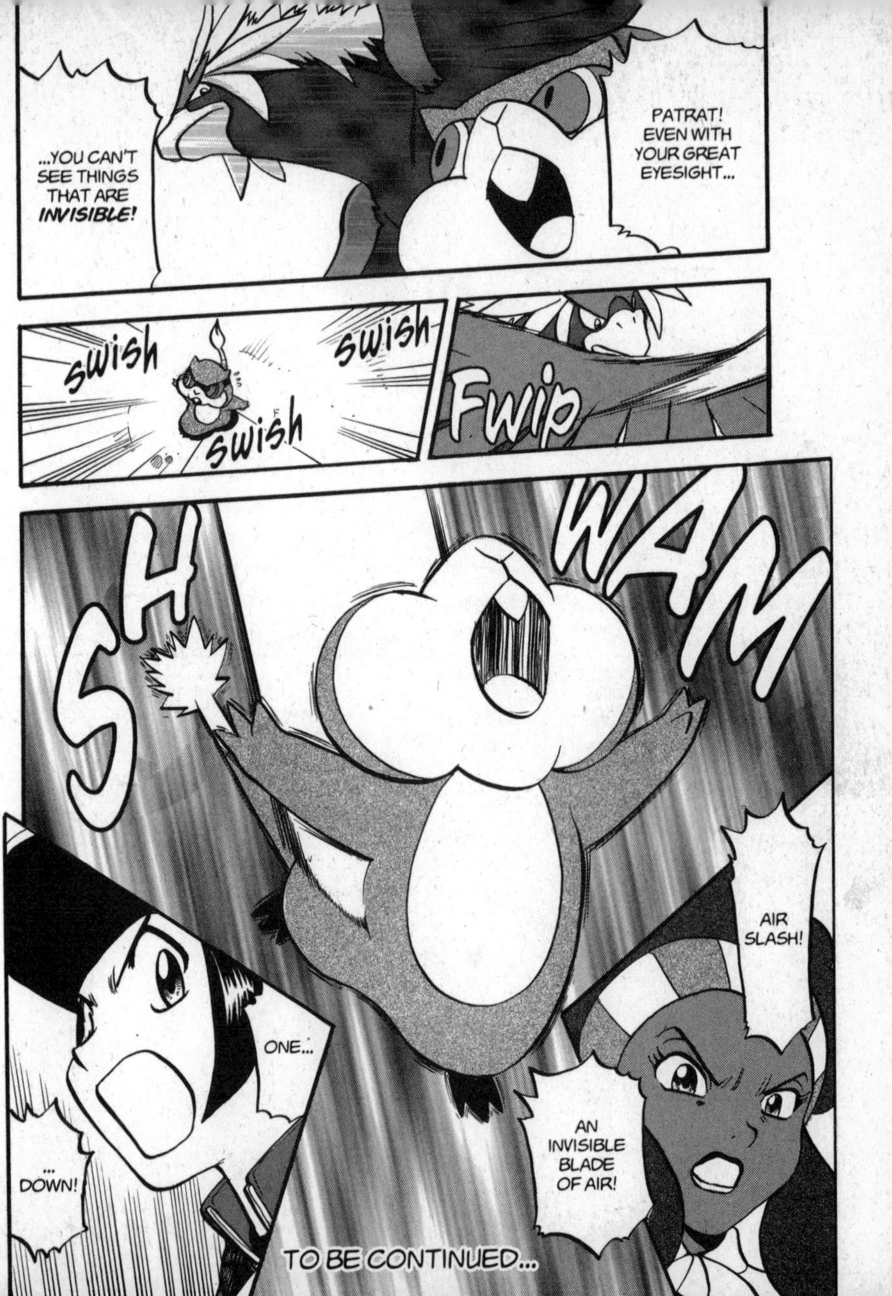
PATRAT! EVEN WITH YOUR GREAT EYESIGHT...
...YOU CAN'T SEE THINGS THAT ARE INVISIBLE!
swish
swish
swish
Fwip
WAM
SH
AIR SLASH!
AN INVISIBLE BLADE OF AIR!
ONE...
... DOWN!
TO BE CONTINUED...

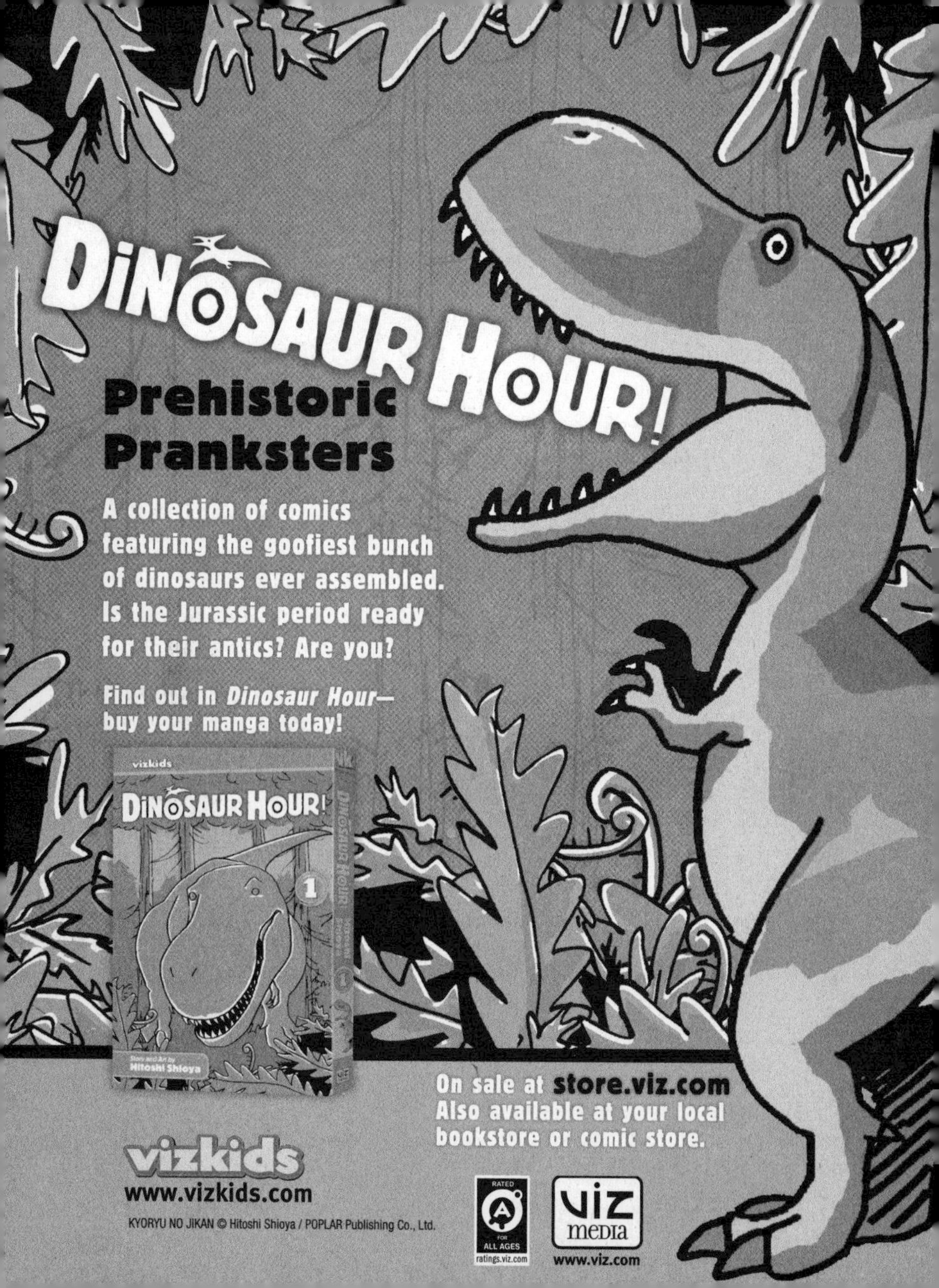
DINOSAUR HOUR!
Prehistoric Pranksters
A collection of comics featuring the goofiest bunch of dinosaurs ever assembled. Is the Jurassic period ready for their antics? Are you?
Find out in Dinosaur Hour—buy your manga today!
vizkids
DINOSAUR HOUR!
1
Story and Art by Hitoshi Shioya
On sale at store.viz.com
Also available at your local bookstore or comic store.
vizkids
www.vizkids.com
KYORYU NO JIKAN © Hitoshi Shioya / POPLAR Publishing Co., Ltd.
RATED
A
FOR ALL AGES
ratings.viz.com
VIZ MEDIA
www.viz.com

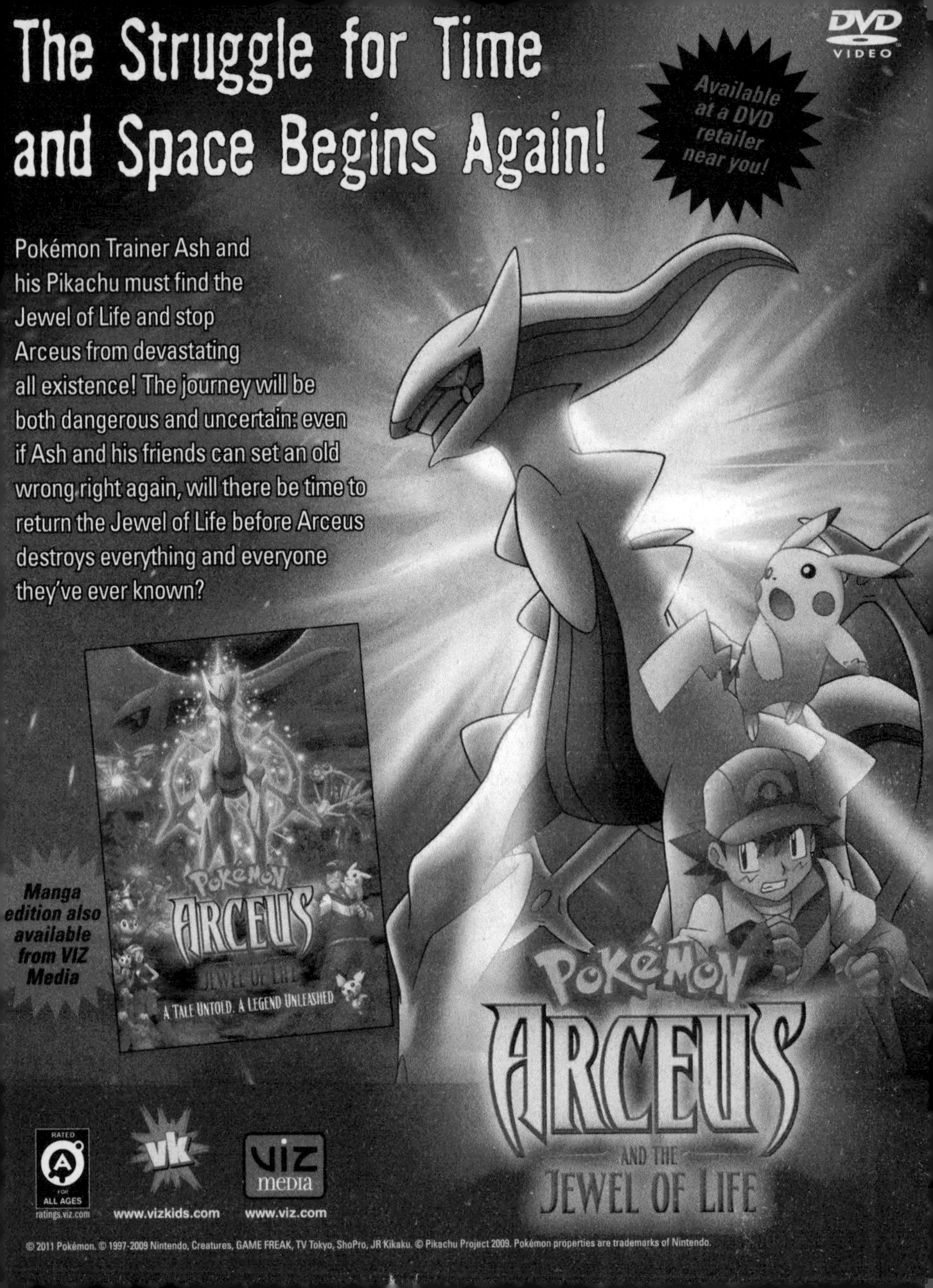
DVD VIDEO
The Struggle for Time and Space Begins Again!
Available at a DVD retailer near you!
Pokémon Trainer Ash and his Pikachu must find the Jewel of Life and stop Arceus from devastating all existence! The journey will be both dangerous and uncertain: even if Ash and his friends can set an old wrong right again, will there be time to return the Jewel of Life before Arceus destroys everything and everyone they've ever known?
Pokémon Arceus Jewel of Life
A Tale Untold, A Legend Unleashed
Manga edition also available from VIZ Media
Pokémon Arceus and the Jewel of Life
RATED A FOR ALL AGES
ratings.viz.com
vk
www.vizkids.com
viz media
www.viz.com
© 2011 Pokémon. © 1997-2009 Nintendo, Creatures, GAME FREAK, TV Tokyo, ShoPro, JR Kikaku. © Pikachu Project 2009. Pokémon properties are trademarks of Nintendo.

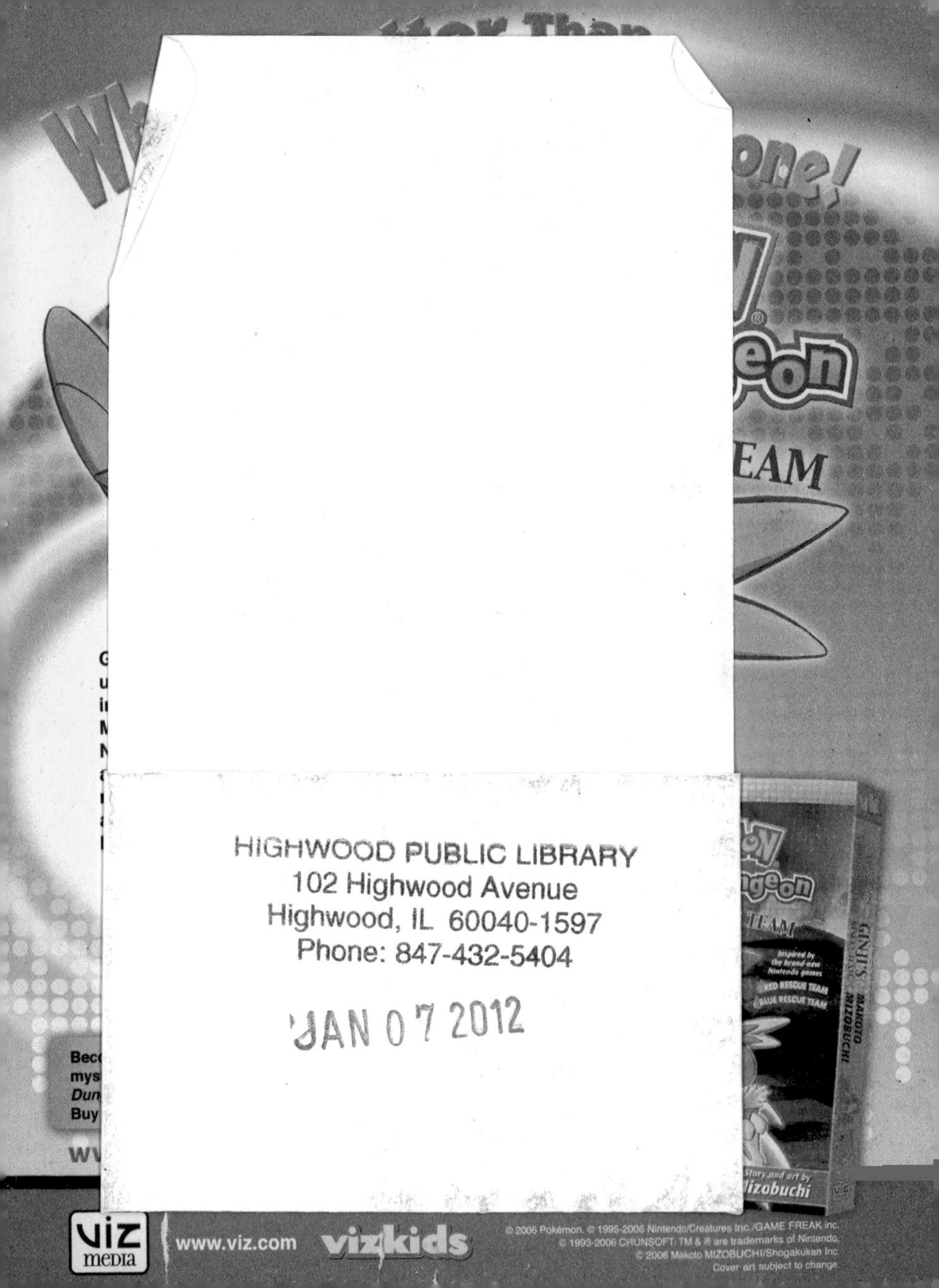
Inspired by the brand-new Nintendo games
RED RESCUE TEAM
BLUE RESCUE TEAM
MAKOTO MIZOBUCHI
Story and art by
Mizobuchi